Jane's Justice

Lyn Bodycoat

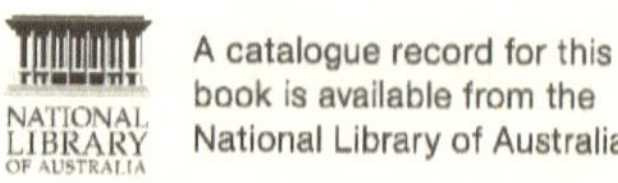

A catalogue record for this book is available from the National Library of Australia

ISBN-13: 978-1-923174-13-9

Linellen Press
265 Boomerang Road
Oldbury, Western Australia
www.linellenpress.com.au

Acknowledgements

I would like to acknowledge the skills, help, and support of members of The Society of Women Writers of WA, particularly Helen Iles, the Chairperson and publisher at Linellen Press.

Reference to places and characters in this book is coincidental as it is a work of fiction. However, like all writing, authors bring their own ideas to the text.

Thank you to friends and family for ideas in the novel's creation.

Contents

Chapter 1

The End of Christmas

The group of cousins sat around the lounge room in Donna and Garry Marshal's home in Port Burnie, on the Eyre Peninsular, South Australia. The idea of eliminating someone hovered in Jane's mind but she fidgeted, unsure whether this was an appropriate time to articulate her thoughts. For now, she pushed the ideas back into the depths of her mind as the group at the party mingled. The lounge room had recently been re-decorated with a stone tile wall enclosing a beautiful fireplace which Garry had bought online and installed himself. Donna, the painter and decorator in the family, prided herself on her attention to detail – each tiny stitch in the curtains had been sewn with love and care. On one wall hung a recent holiday photograph of a charter boat they had sailed around the Greek Islands. Enhancing another wall were large photos of babies, young children, and their parents.

All the cousins were house-proud, clever at decorating for fashion, and spunk. They were in their sixties, with grown-up children, and parents who had passed on. The strong bond they'd had as children had loosened its grip when all their little ones were growing up, but now these youngsters had created their own lives and came with their own families. With the passing of the last aged parent, the cousins rediscovered their connection and quickly rekindled friendships.

'We're like the Greeks really,' said Donna dreamily as she focused on the photo on the wall and sighed – they'd had so much fun together sailing the Mediterranean only a few years earlier. They'd chartered a 40-foot catamaran, Garry's International Skipper's ticket allowing them to sail out of a sleepy fishing village in Greece and embark on a three-week adventure of a lifetime. They had all worked hard and now, with retirement imminent for each of them, they'd felt brave enough to undertake such a mission. It shouldn't have been difficult to plan, but each person had had their own ideas, and no one wanted to flex more muscle than they were entitled to as they lived close to each other and regularly helped each other out.

Donna continued staring at the photo, the memories flowing back to her. 'I can see why ancient mariners became lost whilst travelling all those centuries ago – those fogs become blankets for the unwary. It was a real threat. To stay alert and survive was all part of their daily living. Just imagine surviving the Trojan War, returning home, or at least trying to return home, only to get lost in the fog. How ironic! Who was the sailor who spent years trying to return home to Greece?'

Light shone through the windows and settled on various faces in the room.

'You've been reading too many books,' scoffed Garry. But he instantly took out his phone to google the answer to her query, proudly demonstrating his recently acquired knowledge of the phone.

There were a few suppressed smiles in the group, but put-downs were off-limits. Happy family times together were treasured.

Most knew Greek mythology to some extent, especially Homer and Odysseus, but they let Garry have his moment of glory and nodded when he blurted out the answer. Then the topic of conversation changed.

'When are you returning to your country pad, Bill? Without having to worry about an early harvest, surely you can spend some time in the big smoke.'

'Hmmm … I would love to, but who knows when there'll be some big smoke in the bush … can't fight fires here, mate, living in luxury, though perhaps we'll have to think about moving sooner or later.' Although a retired farmer, Bill remained emotionally invested in the land and still served on his local fire brigade. 'Why don't some of you come to Carinya and visit us? We've got the big festival coming up soon and you lot can help keep me occupied. Bring up your caravans and stay for a while.'

A loud whoop of acceptance rang through the room as another round of drinks arrived on a plastic tray for those who shared the same maternal grandmother. Memories of Nanna Brown running around the house chasing someone with a wooden spoon soon erupted as the drinks flowed into the afternoon. Soon, the idea of a weekend in Carinya, parking the caravans in Bill's driveway or on the vacant lot across the road, drifted into their thoughts. Jane, Bill's wife, nodded agreeably and could almost hear the minds of others ticking over.

Soon enough though, Bill began loading their Landcruiser, preparing for the drive along the hot bitumen roads full of potholes from the recent flooding rains. In the lounge room, Jane kept her head down as she finished the last mouthful of tea. She wanted to focus on this moment, with its warmth and comfort, but deep within her she knew she had words to utter before she left her sister's home. This past year had been such a worry for them and for their son Ryan, his wife being so difficult of late that trauma had visited them in its most nasty form, wreaking havoc on Jane and Bill's mental health.

Jane twisted her wedding ring, and sucked in a deep breath; she squirmed in her chair and ultimately leant forward and blurted out the words to the momentarily quiet group.

'You know, if I had only six months to live, I could easily murder someone.' She took a deep breath and swallowed the lump in her throat. Everyone's jaw dropped open and their eyes widened. Silence invaded the room, giving her time to elaborate.

'Jodie, in effect, left without so much as a word. When Ryan walked in after work a week ago, there it was … a piece of paper on the kitchen bench stating she was staying elsewhere, and little Emily was gone too. Then, in true form, she came back and started playing games, making wild accusations about Ryan. Soon, it was 'game on', unfortunately.'

There, the truth was out. But the lump had risen again to block her throat, those uttered words burning her eyes as tears suddenly spilled over. Then she couldn't speak.

The warm, loving feel in the room suddenly dissipated as Bill took over the explanation. 'Ryan saved up for so long to buy that house, long before he met her, and now it might be sold so she can get half its value. That's years of Ryan's hard work gone. His house will be stolen from him by current family laws.' Bill shook his head and rested his fists on the table. 'He's a heavy diesel mechanic by trade; now he's earning a living as a fisherman with Michael. It's long hours of dirty work in a noisy workshop and on the fishing boat …'

Bill's harsh voice poured out the problem they had, till now, kept hidden. 'Ryan is so lost – she was everything to him – her and little Emily – and now he's wallowing in a pit of distrust and questions. He's in a dark place right now, a real dark place. We just don't know how to reach him.'

Jane's sob escaped as she reiterated her wish. 'I just want to stop his pain …' With her hand clamped over her mouth, suppressing further sounds, she fled the room, brushing past photos of children placed low on tables and delicate glass ornaments that represented domestic harmony. The peace had suddenly shattered as thoughts of manipulation and mistrust intruded into the group.

Bang! The flywire door slammed behind Jane's departure.

She found a seat outside and flopped into it, her hair falling over her face as she dropped her head in her hands in a bid to escape from the world. The sounds of suburbia enveloped her as she slowly regained some composure. Everything had all become too much – what with Ryan's problems with Jodie, and the lingering cough she'd battled for months and recently she'd had morbid thoughts, which she tried to dismiss. Too much was happening all at once.

Soon enough though, she noticed the gentle wind dancing around her, and the smell of jasmine wafted to her nostrils. She heard the door creak open and felt a presence nearby, but let the awkward silence hang in the warm air. Deep in her mind, plotting the demise of her daughter-in-law had given her immense satisfaction. Bill sat down beside her and a fluffy dog cuddled into her legs.

'Don't let her get the better of you, love. This time will pass and so will Ryan's pain. We mustn't let it become our trauma as well or she will destroy us all. Try to think of something else.' Yet Bill's mouth twisted as he uttered those words of comfort.

Jane's shoulders slumped and she heaved in a deep breath. He was right, but how could she eradicate the smell of blood every time Ryan's name and his situation were mentioned?

She heard Bill's hard exhale. He was feeling it too.

'Let's go back inside and help clear up the dishes,' he said. 'Soon we can say our goodbyes and be on the road home. Now the family knows what is happening, we can start to put it behind us.'

Jane glanced across at him, his quiet words doing little to conceal his fury over what that bloody woman had done by infiltrating their son's life and causing them all chaos. *Jesus, how unfair life is. Bill looks exhausted and we have a long drive ahead of us. And now I feel so poorly, he has to deal with me as well. Life is so draining!*

She bent her head low again. 'I can't believe how upset I still become when I think of Jodie. I feel wretched. We were all having such a great time, and then I go and spoilt it by becoming a blubbering mess. Oh well,' she drew in another deep breath, 'at least it's all out in the open now. I didn't realise my fists were so tightly clenched.'

A weak smile spread across Jane's face and her tears dried up as Bill put his arm around her shoulders. He reached inside his pocket, pulled out a used handkerchief.

'Oh yuk. Put that away, you jerk. I'm not using your dirty hanky.'

They both laughed gently and rose to rejoin the group.

Dishes clattered in the sink, and bodies moved around the room, trying to accommodate the discomfort of one of their loved ones. Subdued chatter continued as Jane gathered her belongings for the trip home to Carinya, a two hour drive away. Almost invisibly, an arm slipped around her shoulder, her pain acknowledged and she cherished the comfort of trust in her family. Bill was right: she would have to learn to deal with the pain of her youngest child, who was, after all, a grown man.

*****

Later, Jane and Bill Thompson drove along the familiar, grey, snake-like strip of bitumen that unfolded evenly in front of them, the hum of the engine putting miles behind them. The equally familiar paddocks and dry, scrubby bushes whizzing by outside the windows were part of a vista, hostile to others, but not hostile to them. In the sullen silence, Jane's anger towards her manipulating daughter-in-law resurfaced, and she focused on the way Jodie had maneuvered her way into the family, earned their trust, and was now blowing it away like dust in the paddock. She looked at Bill and wondered how he endured the deception. She sighed. *Maybe he can handle life's complexities better than me.*

Suddenly, in the distance ahead of them, Bill identified a small dot as a police car – the red and blue flashing lights soon visible on the roof were a dead giveaway. They could hear no siren, so it wasn't an emergency, but Bill eased back to well within the speed limit. He hadn't been drinking, but even so, he felt his heart beat faster for just a few moments: a primal reaction to respond to law enforcement with trepidation. He slowed to a stop as he neared the stationary police car.

'Perhaps he's doing random breath tests, or maybe there's been an accident,' he muttered to Jane. Mentally, he prepared himself for scrutiny, making a note in his mind that his license was in his wallet just near him. The policeman glanced Bill's way and walked towards him.

'Afternoon, Bill. I'm just doing random breath tests. I haven't finished setting up yet, so you're off the hook, but the holiday season tends to be a time for manic drivers, and we try to get them off the road. Let's just do a license check to keep my worksheet happy.'

Bill pulled out his driver's licence and handed it to his next-door neighbour. Ned didn't even glance at it – just handed it back and smiled.

'A few more checks and I'll be heading home to watch the cricket. And if you hear a racket after that, it'll be me mowing the Police Station lawn in the cool of the evening … if it ever gets cool.'

He waved Bill on and then attended to his job of setting up a roadside sign – all part of his country policeman's role.

Bill drove on and felt relieved a short time later when the speed limit sign emerged and the sleepy town of Carinya came into view. They could see their home on the edge of town, one house up from the Police Station, separated by the government-provided house of Ned's next door. The sprawling lawn and big gum trees in their yard welcomed them home. The day had been difficult enough and they were thankful to be back, yet felt slightly unsettled as the sun sank behind the lake in the distance.

Red sky at night, shepherd's delight, Jane mused, still at odds with the events of the day. *Surely it isn't an omen.* The thought of Jodie among their beautiful family made her annoyingly uncomfortable again.

Chapter 2

Jane's Diagnosis

Jane gathered up her diary and, during the afternoon, she sat down to record their time away, in particular noting the conversations that had transpired. She snuggled down on the old lounge and made a mental note to clean the fabric soon – it contained the smell of many bodies – lots of people had spread their summer weariness deep within the cushions, as she did now. She'd spent most of yesterday in bed, not that anything was particularly wrong with her, but the thought of Ryan's bad fortune had made her sleep restlessly during the night. Her throat felt tight too, and she thought she might be coming down with a cold.

Flicking through the diary's pages, she realised she was due for her annual check-up. She re-read the words she'd written and, as she looked through the well-worn pages, realised it had been some time since she'd felt totally well. She made a mental note to tell Peg, her doctor, and perhaps she'd check her iron levels. *Perhaps I need to exercise more, like Michael suggested! But I feel so damn tired. And maybe that's because of Ryan's problems. Even psychologists suggest exercise in their trauma counselling and then call it some special name like it's a new discovery!*

They hadn't seen their other son, Michael, for some time now and with Ryan consuming all her maternal energies in recent times, she felt a pang of guilt and realised, once again, how difficult it was to prevent sibling rivalry in her offspring, even at their mature age. *I'll call him soon … when I can muster up some energy,* but for now she concentrated on her diary, encouraging her eyes to focus on the words she'd written.

After a particularly long coughing fit, she phoned the doctor, and sat looking out the window as summer rain softly pattered on the roof, the first drops washing the dust away and giving the plants some much-needed respite from the dry heat. She knew she should mow the lawn before the rain became heavier but … it could wait until she had more spring in her step. Her appointment was scheduled for later in the week. Maybe she would wait till after it to mow the lawn.

Then she remembered to call Michael. He was always busy running work meetings, going fishing, or preparing for the gym, but this time, he answered on the first ring. She frowned that he, too, was feeling 'sluggish'. *Yes, that is how I feel.*

***

Michael was indeed tired – tired of hearing about Ryan's woes, which he believed his brother had brought on himself, to a certain extent. As the older brother, he'd frequently supported his sibling, but now Ryan needed to get a life – he'd disregarded his advice about hooking up with Jodie, and now he was wearing the outcome. He heaved out a deep breath. So what was he supposed to do about it? Perhaps Ryan needed a new job or a trip away somewhere; perhaps he should just get away from it all – the bitch was going to get his house so he might as well accept that fact!

In a new relationship with a chick who intrigued him, Michael had managed so far to keep her at arm's length. Sure, he'd slept with her, but no way was he going to ask her to move in with him. That had been Ryan's weakness – he was needy – and he wanted to do things the right way. That had been his downfall. And that was as much consideration Michael gave the issue. He refocused on getting his next supply of dope, which he was about to head out to pick up.

***

On entering and leaving the pub, an enormous, gloomy, grey building on a busy corner, he scanned the scattering of patrons, trying not to look suspicious while trying to detect any undercover cops. He couldn't be sure of his anonymity and changed his pick-up venue and dealer regularly. *Very risky stuff using the same place too often.* And he didn't want to wear another charge of using.

He refused to accept that he was addicted to the stuff – he was a social user, only using on weekends – though occasionally he lit up after phone calls from his mother, especially when they were all about Ryan. If he ever did become an addict, he would blame Ryan for it, a blatant non-user. His brother's holier-than-thou attitude seriously annoyed him, but for now, he had other things to consider. So he walked steadily to his car to lock his little stash in the glove box. One day, he decided, he would have to start growing his own – it would be cheaper that way – and then maybe he would entertain sharing it with Sharon. Sex was so much better when he was high.

***

On arriving home from the pub, Michael changed clothes, combed his hair and prepared for work. He wasn't sure why he cared about his appearance when, in half an hour or so, he'd be out on the boat hauling up the evening's catch. But then, perhaps he'd see some chicks on the way to the marina – who knows? He shut the front door loudly and stepped out to his car parked in the driveway.

This time of year was pleasant, most of the summer heat had dissipated, thank goodness, which meant more time on the boat fishing as the late afternoon breezes subsided. Late evening catches tended to be more productive with less heat in the day, and it was important to keep up his catch numbers so he could pay off his recently acquired 12-metre boat and professional fishing licences. He could have gone out early in the morning, but it was harder to find a morning crew, and each time he headed out he needed a crew of three or four to bait the lines and drop the pots.

Motley young blokes and middle-aged men mingled around as he approached the dock. And there was his beautiful boat, just waiting for him to unlock the cabin so the crew could prepare the pots and assume their roles.

'Let's go, guys, and get away quick towards Boggy Bay. If the breeze stays non-existent, we should be able to get in close to the reef.'

A few others milled around the boat ramp as they cast off, and he scanned the activity out of interest. *Mainly walkers undertaking some token exercise to make them feel good*, he decided. *Honestly, some folk take this measure too seriously.* It seemed pointless to Michael, but, being sociable at heart, he called out greetings to all he knew. He scanned further, looking for any good-looking girls, but they usually didn't hang around a place like this; they were more inclined to be found in the pub or strolling along the beachfront. So Michael nosed the boat out and headed towards Boggy Bay, the crew busy cutting meat to lure the crays with their primal need for food. Baiting the pots and lines was so routine each crewman knew his role and acted accordingly, ensuring they would be paid at the end of the week.

'Don't forget to sign the paysheet when it comes around, and indicate if you're available for an early morning shift,' Michael shouted above the roar of the diesel engines. 'I only need one or two crew for the morning run.' *Most will be sleeping off hangovers at 4 am anyway*, he half grinned.

No one answered; the engine roar was too loud, and the waves crashing against the boat ensured voices were drowned out anyway. He could manage with only one person if he had to, but it was easier if two managed the pots and lines while he managed the boat.

All too soon, they dropped pots in their favourite locations, located by landmarks rather than GPS. Eventually, the boat slowly idled towards the marina pen. No one was in sight now, the bystanders having left and were probably at home having their dinner in front of the television.

'See you guys in the morning,' Michael called out as his crew left the boat. He had two accepting the four o'clock run to pull up the pots, an easy enough job at this time of the year when the breezes were mild or dead. Soon the season would close for the winter, and these two old-timers could sleep in.

Now in his late thirties, Michael considered himself an old-timer too, especially now he was busy paying off his boat and his house.

As he unlocked his front door, he noticed his mobile phone flashing and looked down at the screen. It was his mother. *Oh no, not more of Ryan's sob story*, he thought. He let it ring out. Maybe he would contact her later.

***

'He's not responding,' Jane muttered when Bill entered the kitchen from outside. 'I'll try again later but he should be home after dropping off his pots. Perhaps he's gone out again?'

'Or perhaps he's in the middle of something. Anyway, come and sit down. I think we need a bit of time before we tell him anyway.'

Jane allowed herself to be led to a chair then Bill cleared away their dinner dishes. Peg's words in the doctor's surgery rolled around in her head, starting off as a murmur but steadily increasing until the words screamed at her in disbelief – words like 'shadow, cell multiplication, cancer, limited treatment!' What did this all mean? She had presented with symptoms of lethargy and coughing.

'But x-rays and blood tests don't lie,' had been Peg's response when Jane receded into denial mode. Luckily, Bill had sat beside her so all she had to do was process the conversation. She vaguely heard Peg's words to Bill about chemotherapy and how it would lengthen her life. This had been a brutal conversation, but Jane realised doctors didn't dance around these facts, which need to be imparted to patients in the clearest way possible, and with as much sensitivity and diplomacy as one could muster. After all, Peg and Jane had known each other for many years, and it couldn't have been easy for Peg to witness her patient's tears of horror and shock. From now on, Jane would see an oncologist in Port Burnie for her treatment.

'A cup of tea doesn't change anything, but it might make you feel better,' Bill muttered as he handed Jane the soothing liquid. He, himself, felt like emptying a flagon of whiskey but knew he had to be strong for his wife.

Jane took the tea and slid it down on her little table beside her lounge chair. She let it cool down before taking a sip. 'You're right. It does make me feel a bit better. But the nausea in my stomach just wants to make me heave.' She sat, staring into space, seeing her life playing out and the family's reaction to the news. Time and silence hung in the air. 'Let's not say anything to anyone for a while.'

'I agree.'

Then they each sat there in their own world of bewilderment as the kitchen clock ticked knowingly. Their world of menace was about to begin though neither of them knew it until they fully processed Peg's words and started to accept the inevitability of the human world. 'We'll let the boys know first.'

Subsequently, Michael ignored his mother's phone call.

Jane would call him later and she braced herself for what she had to say. She felt herself relax as the phone went unanswered and she hung up before it went to voice mail. He'd ring back when he was ready.

After another sleepless night, morning eventually came to the quiet town of Carinya and it began the same as any other day, with cups of tea, bacon and eggs. Then the process of sitting began. Before too long, the phone rang, and Michael's cheery voice came over the line – thoughts of his parents and their comfy home in the country always made him cheerful. While it wasn't too far from the coast and his home, it wasn't close enough to visit for a meal.

Michael's silence registered his disbelief. He couldn't believe what his father had told him and instantly demanded, 'Get another opinion!'

Bill firmly repeated Peg's words about X-rays and blood tests. Finally, the words 'I'll come down on the weekend' echoed through the air long after the call had disconnected. Bill soon realised that coping with Jane was one thing, but coping with others would soon present its own challenges. Oh well, it wasn't long to wait until the weekend. He guessed he'd better tell Ryan so the two boys could come together for a visit in a few days to process the dreadful news.

Chapter 3

Jodie and Ryan

Jodie dumped the dirty dishes in the sink, the heavy plates clattering as she sloshed them around in the suds. She stopped, her hands immersed in the hot water as she stared out the window, her thoughts darkening again as she dwelt on the state of her marriage to *The Loser*. He was a fit, good-looking man and she had loved his ready smile and beautiful blue eyes when they'd first met, but now he was boring. He'd become so predictable, and all he did was work and play, work and play sport ... *God, he's so tedious!* ... So tedious, she deliberately picked arguments, any argument, just to get some sort of spark from him. Ryan had likened her behaviour to crossing a border into a strange land, one he didn't know how to navigate. Then he simply stopped travelling, not coming home to cross any borders until he absolutely had to.

She thumped another dish into the sink, felt it connect with others, heard the chink as it chipped. *And Ryan is puzzled by my strange behaviour? Alright, so others would kill to have a steady husband who shares household chores and plays with the kids, but I need more than that in my life.* She'd gone looking for it with other men.

Her latest acquisition – which was how she saw her flings – resembled Ryan in appearance, and a smile spread as she remembered the shape and firmness of his chest as he'd pinned her down amongst the bushes. She liked the mystique of the unknown, and the excitement of screwing a near stranger in the local forest thrilled her. She recalled how deeply he'd kissed her … …

Suddenly the back door banged as Emily arrived home from school. That marked the end of Jodie's daydreaming … *until next time*. Despite feeling aroused at the thought of her new lover, she turned her attention to her daughter.

'When can I stay at Grandma's house again?' the little girl asked.

Jodie wasn't sure how to answer that. In her mind, she had intentions of announcing the end of her marriage again when Ryan came home from work, and the contact between her daughter and her mother-in-law, Jane, would become extremely limited, if there was any contact at all. She knew exactly what she was going to say to Ryan – she'd been married before so this wasn't new ground for her – and she'd told Ryan numerous times that she wanted to leave him. And now it was time.

Taking a deep breath, Jodie pulled out a chair and sat down next to her daughter.

***

'Mum, I don't know how to say this,' Ryan blurted out one day when he knew he couldn't put it off any longer. His mother had been giving him strange looks, knowing looks, and he knew he'd lost the spring in his step and couldn't fake it any more. Taking a deep breath, he sat down next to Jane, wondering how he could break it to her gently. 'Mum,' he said pointedly, 'I guess you know something is going on …'

She looked at him but didn't answer.

'Jodie is leaving me … she wants out of our marriage.'

Jane wrapped her hands tighter around her cup. 'Thought something was up,' she said bluntly, looking at the liquid swirling from her stirring.

Ryan stared into his cup. 'She's been saying for a while she wants out … It's going to happen soon, I can feel it. We hardly touch each other anymore and when I try to love her, she pushes me away. She's told me several times she wants me to leave.'

'What do you mean, son? … she wants *you* to leave? But it's *your* house!'

Ryan's hands raked hard through his hair, then he held his head tightly, pressuring his temples. 'Jodie knows the Family Court system. She even told me the courts generally support the women … the mothers … retain the family home … and get this … 'particularly when husbands have alcohol issues and are abusive." Ryan shook his head, defeated.

'But you hardly drink, love.'

'I know. One beer a night –that's it. And the only time I got angry with her was when she blew all my pay on stuff we didn't need. That's not abuse – that's just an argument.'

'Oh, love,' was all Jane could say.

'She even said she knows she will gain sympathy in court during our divorce because she knows how the system works. She's been through it before with Callum.' Ryan shook his head again and lowered his head. 'I should have listened to him when he told me she'd fabricated everything. He'd never hit her, not once, and he didn't have a drinking problem either. Hell, I should have listened. I should have listened!'

'What about Emily, Ryan? What's going to happen to Emily?'

Staring straight ahead, Ryan shook his head, and when he looked across at her, tears filled his eyes. 'I don't know, Mum. I don't know.'

'Well, you just hang in there, love. Don't ever leave that house or she will have it whipped out from under you. Just stick to your guns – let her be the one to leave. That way you will have a roof over Emily's head.'

***

It wasn't long before Emily didn't visit very much, and Jane knew it was because of Jodie. She hadn't warmed to Jodie from the first day they'd met –there was just something about her – but she'd trusted her son's judgement and respected his choices. She had expected her adult children would grow distant as they matured and had filled the gap they left with Ryan's daughter. But this separation, this divorce, whatever it was to be, would mean distance from Emily too.

***

Time went on, and Jane toddled about with her daily routine but gone was the smile she used to have not so many years ago. Ryan's emotional pain and the loss of her contact with Emily filled her with despair, then indifference, and then an unnatural kind of hatred permeated her thinking. One day, Jane felt her fists clench and realised demonic thoughts were filling her mind. They led to daydreams and fantasies, and soon, though sensitive and intelligent, Jane's hatred for Jodie festered. Plans formed in her mind, starting out as ideas, and she soon began to wonder how to turn them into reality.

She eventually turned to Bill.

***

Remembering how stoic Bill had been when dealing with her medical diagnosis, how he had told their children and, despite them being adults, dealt with their childlike demands of 'Did you get a second opinion? Perhaps the tests were wrong!', he had handled everything. Eventually, a subtle quietness reigned, and the numbness of acceptance crept into their souls until everyone became positive. But Jane knew chemotherapy only brought her time; it wasn't a cure. The children were not fooled either. Right now though, she needed Bill's help with this situation.

She stared out the window as the lawn mower roared to life, Bill reluctantly tackling the lawn that she used to do. To what point, Jane sometimes wondered.

After dinner, when they both sat in the lounge watching television, Jane knitting as usual, her courage rose, even though she suspected her plan would not be readily embraced.

'I just want to eliminate that bitch Jodie,' Jane began, planning to slowly work up to the reasons for this primal action – Bill's idea of 'eliminating' might have a sanitised version. 'There's no kind way out of this situation for Ryan. Jodie has betrayed him, ruined him, taken our granddaughter.

'Do you think $20,000 is about the right figure for a hit? You know, a ballpark figure?' She kept her head down, concentrated on her knitting as though she hadn't spoken.

Bill's loud guffaw caused her to raise her head, then he looked serious. 'Jane! You've got to be joking!' His mouth opened and closed a few times as he searched for other words, but none came.

She feigned absolute surprise. 'Of course, I was joking. You don't really think ...' She forced a chuckle. Went back to her knitting. 'Of course, I was kidding. But oh, how that would save our situation.' The knitting needles clicked and clacked on and on, the TV show droned in the background, Bill's flapping mouth soon settling into a slow smile. He shook his head as he looked across at her, rattled by her thinking. She almost sighed, knowing he wouldn't be party to it, but, as she'd intended, she'd planted the seed.

They both knew if Jodie divorced Ryan, he would lose the home he'd worked so hard to buy. He'd paid off most of the mortgage before he'd even met her, but a divorce would see him homeless and devastated. Depression had already set in at the prospect of losing Jodie, and now the prospect of losing everything he had worked for, and his daily contact with his previous little Emily. Jodie, the henchman and ruler, had become even bolder, demanding now that he leave the house; she'd even started packing his things. And Emily was wrapped up in the middle, powerless at eight years old to have any input into the decisions being made. *How unfair was that for her*, Jane often thought. *She will grow up missing Ryan and missing us.*

She thought about the money they had sitting in the bank, just sitting there doing nothing – money from the sale of the farm that was half hers – money that she would sooner than later have no use of because she wouldn't be here. There was enough sitting in the account that Bill wouldn't even notice a portion of it gone, and she did the accounts – she just had to stay well enough to keep doing the accounts. *Is $20 grand enough though?* She'd seen shows on TV about hitmen for hire … professionals might cost more, but sleaze-bags like those who attend the annual bike show and Speedway would probably do it for less. She just had to know how to approach one.

The more she thought about it, the more determined she became. It would be a godsend to her if her one final act was saving Ryan from that bitch he had married.

She noted Bill occasionally glancing across at her, his mouth opening and closing as though he wanted to say something but was hesitant, the TV show no longer enough to occupy his thoughts. She had definitely rattled his cage, and now she had to pacify him, and most certainly, she couldn't rely on him to help her work through this. She smiled nonchalantly, the first step in letting him forget what she'd said.

Bill heaved a deep sigh. 'Jane, let's take our tea out in the garden and watch the sunset.'

And so, they sat on the verandah in the old wicker chairs they'd purchased many years ago, chairs that had heard many family stories on the verandah at the farm. This time the chairs had to be satisfied with sharing Bill's and Jane's thoughts – their words holding too many fears for the future. Bill's white sideburns and salt-and-pepper hair framed his long, lean, pixie-shaped face that now had a stillness creeping along the lines that had only just started appearing. They had begun at a crawl, but life recently had accentuated their spread at a surprisingly rapid rate. He wore black shorts and a sleeveless shirt for daily work these days, no need for the long dungarees he wore on the farm, but when the sun was fierce, he donned his old straw hat to provide shade for his eyes. As he sipped his black tea, he heaved another sigh.

'Listen, love, I think the drugs are affecting your thoughts,' he finally said. 'You might need to rest more for this crazy idea to go out of your head.'

He studied her face to assess her previous words as mere senseless ramblings and found her smile shielded by her lowered head a little comforting. Then she chuckled again and looked up.

'I told you I was kidding, Bill. Don't go on about it … and I'm sorry if I scared you – I didn't mean to. It was just a nice thought to get me over this pain of watching Ryan suffer.'

Bill exhaled loudly and nodded. 'Alright. However, you need to cope, love, as long as they are just thoughts.'

Jane nodded her assurance, and her whole body relaxed. She closed her eyes for a few moments, overriding a slight nagging pain that was building in her side. She focused intently on the sunset, which seemed to glow a dark red as if the forces of nature were on her side.

***

Both Bill and Jane knew the implications of a metastasised cancer. How this was going to play out Bill couldn't even imagine, and he didn't want to think about it. Jane's time to leave this earth was approaching and she was accepting this better than other family members. While he, too, hated his daughter-in-law with a passion and wanted her gone, he wasn't prepared to even contemplate such an action as Jane. *Maybe she's been watching too many of those murder shows. Maybe the drugs are affecting her mind.* Yet he mused how easy it was to eliminate noxious weeds and plants – and Jodie had become toxic – but this sort of elimination was beyond thinking about. He couldn't help staring at the garden's grey concrete path along which a tiny ant carried its huge load. He wondered if tiny creatures had problems like humans, but decided their lives were simpler. He pondered over the load of an ant and compared it with the new load on his shoulders. To snuff out this ant's life, all he had to do was walk down the path, but which path had to be navigated for Ryan's survival? And which for Jane's? *Did she realise what she was asking? Was it just a way for her to cope? What was she thinking? Or was she really joking?* But the thoughts would not abate no matter how hard he tried to shift them from his mind.

He didn't want to take away the life of the hard-working ant on his garden path, so he certainly would never organise a hit on his granddaughter's mother. Of course not! He straightened his back and glanced again at Jane, intending to tell her again to shelve those thoughts for good. But he saw the rays of happiness shining from her face and realised she was at peace.

She was dying and he didn't want to distress her by pushing the issue again, so he let it go. Pushed away that she had ever said such a thing, even in jest.

***

Nothing was mentioned in their household again on the matter and days, weeks, passed with each locked in their own private reveries. Bill enjoyed the silence, while Jane actively planned how to distance Bill from her activities, which would have huge ramifications on the family after her passing if she was found out. It wasn't possible at this stage of her illness to increase her pain medication so she fumbled around in silent pain as best she could, carrying out her daily chores at a snail's pace while her mind ran a deadly marathon. As time passed, with the rituals of eating and living, each separated into a paradigm of their own, the hours, the minutes, both day and night, slipped away in the screaming quietness of moments, as the earth spun on its axis towards a one-way existence for all its inhabitants.

Chapter 4

A Visit to the Bank

The red and white building in the small country town beckoned her on that autumn day as Jane walked down the path towards it. She and Bill had known Stan, the manager, for years and today Jane had mentally prepared what she would say in her appointment. Yes, it had to be an appointment! She'd be making a large cash withdrawal, which she'd had to organise ahead of time as the bank didn't always carry a huge amount of cash. Stan had said he'd have it ready for her when she came in, and today was the day. She was taking out just below the amount the bank would need explanations for to the various government departments, and not quite enough to raise eyebrows or cause Stan concern. *Hell, we have heaps in the account, this little bit will go unnoticed, and Bill never checks the accounts – that's my domain, my role in the family ... the Income and Expenditure Manager.* Even though she was nervous, she almost chuckled, but deliberately avoided looking up at the CCTV camera as the bank's heavy door closed behind her. She didn't know why; she wasn't guilty of anything ... *well, not yet.*

Stan stood outside his office in the bank, sipping on a cup of coffee. 'Right on time, Jane!' he greeted her amicably. 'I reckon I could set my watch by you. But then again, I'm like that too. I received a watch for my tenth birthday and have been obsessive about time ever since.'

'Stan ...' Jane smiled. '... that's what makes you good at your job!'

'Come on in, and we can have a look at your accounts and see if there is anything else we can do for you. This shouldn't take long.'

Jane sat on the edge of her seat and straightened her blouse. Dressing appropriately for formal meetings had always been important to her, and she figured this was an important meeting. *I'm just tying up loose ends,* she told herself, *justifying the actions that will be disastrous when I'm not here to face questions from the authorities.* Ultimately, the conversation started.

'As I said before, I would like to withdraw $9,500 from the holding account, in cash. I'm going to put it safely away to help Michael pay for his boat, when the time is right. Then, in a few months, when I may not be very well, I will withdraw the same amount, in cash, for Ryan. It'll be a great surprise for them and might bring a little ray of brightness for them when my illness grows worse. Both boys could do with the extra funds, so I figured, why not pay them sooner than later? It might bring a little brightness for me, too, when I see the joy on their faces.'

Indeed, she had thought about leaving a large amount of her financial assets to Michael and Ryan and had imagined their surprise and happy faces.

Stan nodded with understanding. 'Why not, indeed, Jane? It will be a lovely gesture. We have that amount in cash ready for you. Is it coming out of your own account, or the holding account? Let's open this computer and have a look at your accounts. And we'll put in a request for the same amount for next week.' He pressed the intercom to the outside counter. 'Rhonda, can you bring in that special order for Mrs Thompson.'

A moment later, the young teller, her friend Carol Jessop's daughter, entered and laid a long envelope on Stan's desk.

When she left the room, Stan opened the envelope and counted out the cash, all in $100 bills.

'Thanks, Stan,' Jane said, and stowed the thick, sealed bank envelope into her purse. 'After Ryan's amount, I'll do a similar surprise for Bill. He never does anything nice for himself, you know. It's time he reaps some rewards as well. Shine some brightness after all the bad times he's been going through with me. You know what I mean.' She looked Stan straight in the eyes, willing him to pick up on the word 'surprise'. For it to be a surprise, he'd not be able to say anything to any of them. A shudder crept up her spine on realising how she'd carried this off. *How horribly deceitful I am* prodded her. But it was too late now, she had the first instalment in her purse. *Only two more amounts to collect and I'll be ready, provided I can get it done for this amount.*

With her business all done, Jane left the bank, Stan escorting her to her car. 'I am so sorry for your health situation, Jane, and I admire your fortitude in putting your affairs in order while you can,' he said.

Though pain was starting to build behind her ribs, she smiled and drew a tight breath. 'I don't want any lawyer trying to sort out my affairs – they'll just chew up the family inheritance!' She slid into the driver's seat. 'I'll see you in a week for Ryan's gift.'

***

Jane's friend Fay was out the back of her home when Jane rang the front doorbell. Jane knew Fay didn't work this day of the week so she'd be able to have a private conversation with the friend she'd known for many years.

'What's up, my friend? Not that you need a reason to visit!' Fay said brightly. 'Come in and I'll put the kettle on. How are you feeling today?'

'I'm coping, Fay, for the moment. The chemo knocks me for a six though. Spend days in bed after it … just lay there thinking about the end and what it will be like. I think I might need an extra strong coffee today.'

Midway to the fridge, Fay stopped and looked back at Jane; she rested her hand on her friend's shoulder, understanding. 'However it is, Jane, I know you. You are strong. You will cope.'

'I'm going to be straight with you, Fay – I am scared stiff. But that's not what I came for today.' And here came the second great deception. 'Bill and I are having a discussion … a very pointed discussion. You and John have lived in Carinya for some time now … so … who would you consider is the most corrupt or connected resident in town if you know what I mean.'

'Criminally you mean?' Fay clarified. She frowned then half smiled, and pulled the milk bottle out of the fridge. 'Including or discluding your lovely neighbour Ned Lawson.'

Jane's head spun her way. 'Ned?' Her jaw dropped open.

'Rumour has it he's very well 'connected'.' Fay slid the coffee cups onto the table. 'And I wouldn't be surprised. You've only got to look at how chummy he is with the low-lifes who attend the Speedway event. Right chummy he is with them … which I find quite disturbing with him being a cop.'

Jane half-forced a laugh. No, she couldn't ask Ned. Not at all. 'I never go to the speedway – it's too noisy; too full of those bikie types …' but that was who she needed in all of this. 'Apart from Ned,' she finally added.

'Well, you've got creepy Carl from the shire …'

'The one who runs the bar?'

'Yep. Slimy and as connected as they come. John and I reckon he makes ten times more with the 'other' deals he makes at the event on top of selling the beer. And then there's old man Ferguson's son, we call him Feral.'

'Glynn? He used to be Michael's best mate.'

'Yep. We reckon he's growing dope out on his old man's farm. See him regularly in town or on the road meeting up with those bikie types … probably selling his crop. And old man Ferguson wouldn't have a clue.' Fay sipped her drink as Jane wondered if that was how Michael started smoking dope. She hoped he had now stopped, though doubted it.

'We think Ned knows what's going on, but does nothing to stop it. Maybe he's on the take.'

Jane's eyebrows rose. Had she had blinkers on the whole time they'd been living in the town?

Fay was on a roll. 'John and I call the annual speedway event a trade fair – you only have to look at the roughnecks that ride into town to know they are not here exclusively for the car racing. Most of them would probably cut their mother's throats without blinking an eye over it.' Fay's smile spread.

Jane's smile widened, and her eyes glimmered. *Could it possibly be so easy?* 'Maybe I need to go to the speedway this year. Watching what's going on on the sidelines might be more interesting than what's on the track,' she laughed. Inside, her stomach bubbled with excitement. *How easy this could be. I just have to get Bill to take me to the speedway.*

'John will be involved again this year, helping to manage the venue, and I'll be going to help him. We might see you there then.'

Jane nodded but inwardly decided she would need to keep a low profile from her friend if she was there.

'So, what's the real reason for needing this information?' Fay asked her bluntly, her friend's eyes now hard and penetrating.

Jane looked up in shock. *She's onto me. How did that happen? Think. Think quick.* Then she remembered a conversation she'd had with Bill. 'I need someone, one of those lowlifes maybe, to sell me some of that marijuana stuff. Michael told Bill it would help me through when the painkillers don't work so well, and I don't want to ask Michael to get me some when he's got off the stuff. And I wouldn't want to get him into trouble.' Jane's lip trembled as she murmured these words, yet she felt surprised that her voice didn't quiver. Her gaze dropped to the floor, and for a moment she sat silent. Then she sucked in a breath and said, 'Fay, I'm on limited time … nothing is working … the cancer's too aggressive. I just need to have things in place to make it as easy as possible, and I surely don't want to fall apart in front of my kids.'

She had chosen her words and reasons carefully.

Fay looked out the kitchen window to the front street where rubbish was being removed from her verge. She shook her head at Jane's request. 'I know you are in a lot of pain, Jane. But is this what you really want to do? What if you get caught …?'

Bugger! I'm desperate, and Fay might help, but within legal limits. This could be a problem, Jane realised.

Both women sipped their coffee. Nothing more needed to be said, and any conversation for now would be surplus to requirement. Jane felt pleased Fay had pointed her in the right direction and suddenly, overwhelmingly, felt that life was going to be okay. From now on, she could feel contented, as long as she could get Bill to take her to the speedway. She'd just need to slip away, maybe approach Creepy Carl for a contact and go from there. She had the first wad of money and arranged to get the second. She would have it by the time the speedway came to town. She felt good and suddenly found it easy to focus on the banal and mundane. Conversations about the weather had never sounded so good, and yes, indeed, the future looked bright. *Mission accomplished,* she thought as she stepped outside sometime later and walked towards her car.

Grey clouds had thickened in the sky and it looked like rain approaching, Jane realised as she stepped over and onto old brown dead leaves. *Some parts of nature have given up and withered.* She didn't mind crunching old leaves underfoot, but she wouldn't step on new vegetation encroaching close to the path. Some aspects in life, and in death, needed to be dealt with, and Jane was on a mission – a successful mission so far.

She stopped at the local shop and bought some special treats for their dinner, chatting this day with her favourite, always cheerful, checkout lady about the current decline in dress standards of young people. The woman complimented Jane on her choice of food items as she busily pushed them through the checkout and towards the shopping bags – chicken curry was Bill's favourite and it had been some time since she'd been able to put effort into anything really, so tonight was going to be a treat! Since her diagnosis, she'd been living in shock and consumed with every little ache and pain. Her oncologist told her the pain would be minimal 'at this stage', but it was the final three words that scared her most. Her initial response was to count days and then months. Her nights were regularly consumed with dreams of situations she could not escape from, and her counsellor had provided her with strategies to help her cope. Sometimes, she found herself reading or watching television in the wee small hours of the morning. Often music helped.

Sitting at the kitchen table that night, Bill looked at her fondly and she sensed his relief was from her positive spirit.

Little did he know her good spirits were the result of the conversation with Fay and her plan coming to some kind of reality. No longer was it just an idea prodding her mind.

That night, she slept like a drunken pig and woke refreshed – the first time in many months.

Chapter 5

Michael's Life

Michael's home, an old weatherboard house just a short distance from the marina, matched his lifestyle perfectly. He'd bought the place quite cheap and its ramshackle garden and shoddy appearance suited him. He believed shabbiness hid any pretence of keeping up with neighbours who were keen on street appeal for their land values. He wasn't bothered by material values, such as real estate and renovations, and hated the whole idea of creating a good-looking house. *Who cares?* he reasoned.

It was different with his fishing boat though … well, the fishing boat he shared with Ryan. And he was just as intent on maintaining good catches. As long as he could earn enough to maintain his lifestyle, he was happy. Sure, extra funds made life easier, and he still had a massive overdraft on his share of the boat, but he was currently keeping up his monthly payments with a comfortable enough surplus to buy his dope. His small circle of friends had similar interests, and their love of the ocean created a bond of seadogs together.

As he'd told one of his drinking mates at the pub one night, 'My parents have helped me and Ryan out. We didn't want to become farmers like Dad so they eventually sold up the farm and moved into town. They bought a house and invested in creating a fishing business for us. No way was I going to work my guts out on the land while climate change is killing everything. You watch the skies every day praying for rain … watching your crops and sheep die … nope, not for me. Not for Ryan. Life on the sea is a much better alternative.'

'Where you still watch the skies for rain …' his friend had reminded him. They'd both laughed.

Indeed, month after month, as the seasons unfolded, and the winds blew fiercely or whispered in their passing, many crayfish ended their lives feeding humans and pumping dollars into Michael and Ryan's pockets. The sun, too, either warmed blisteringly or didn't shine in the depth of winter. Although the fishing was important, sometimes maintenance was more important, and this had to coincide with non-fishing times – generally mid-winter, and while slipway time could be bought, it had to be managed strategically to maximise profits. After all they had fuel, marina fees and wages to pay each week, and the crew expected to be paid on time, which, he shrugged, was fair and reasonable. The licence covered seven days a week and didn't have restrictions. The boat was a big investment, nearly a million dollars, but Ryan had a half share in the boat, and he guessed his mum and dad too as they had laid down a hefty deposit. Bill's favourite saying was: 'As long as people eat, we'll have an income.'

As Michael walked briskly along the jetty, he could see Ryan adjusting the winches and checking the ropes and pots. 'All okay?' he asked.

Ryan didn't look up; they just kept working on the pots. 'Yep. Three crew today and a new bloke starting tomorrow. Bit of a light breeze coming from the south so let's get this thing moving. The sooner we get out, the sooner we get home. Breeze could come up a bit later.'

Ryan had always been keen to leave the dock early, or at least on time, believing the mechanical checking could be done on the way and the crew could start baiting up. No good having deckhands standing around being idle – that just gave them time to become bored and complain.

'For sure,' replied Michael as he swung onto the deck. They were men of few words: Michael tended to the operational side of the business; Ryan took care of the mechanical side.

Just before Michael started the engines, he saw old Jack limping up the jetty towards them, waving his arms to attract attention. *Oh, what does he want!* Michael thought, and yelled out, 'Here's trouble. What's up, Jack?'

'New girl on the weighbridge tonight so no freebies for this little boat tonight,' he sniggered as he rubbed his beard and leant against a jetty post. *Poor old bloke's battling*, thought Michael, but he knew Jack was no slouch; he knew his stuff.

'What do you mean, Jack?'

'You know what I mean! Anyway, Jodie's just called in sick so I had to get relief staff to do the weighing of the catch. Just saying … … no big deal. Or it shouldn't be a big deal for you two!' This was his silent warning to Michael and Ryan about keeping the books in proper order and not fudging numbers in the weighing process. Jodie usually managed to adjust the figures to their advantage, usually adding a few kilos to each consignment sent in for processing.

'I had the pleasure of seeing your truckload at the weighbridge today,' Jodie would say. 'I just added a few extra kilos to your catch.'

'Don't do that, Jodie,' Ryan would say but he knew Jodie took no notice of anyone, let alone her husband. 'You'll lose your job and we'll lose our contract and possibly be charged with a crime. A fine will see us on the wrong side of the law, and you're committing fraud as well as stealing.'

'You don't appreciate anything I do,' Jodie had yelled back at him, and an argument would ensue. She flaunted the law frequently, which worried Ryan no end. He hadn't disclosed this to Michael, but this time Michael wanted to know what Jack was talking about.

Ryan simply shrugged and sat down on the boat's bait box, planning what he needed to say next.

'I think Jodie's getting sick of me,' he said when Jack had gone on his way. 'And I guess I'm getting sick of her too. Last night she told me she was leaving me but it's not the first time she's made those kinds of noises. Lately, she's been clearing out for the night; she stays somewhere … I don't know where … or care. But sure enough, she's home when I finish work, cooking dinner, like nothing had happened.'

Michael didn't like to tell Ryan he'd seen Jodie drive off with the truckie who'd taken their catch to the processing plant on several occasions. He'd put it down to Jodie needing a lift somewhere at first, but it had happened frequently lately and Michael had started thinking she was up to some hanky panky.

'Look, mate, you know what these women are like. She might just need a break.'

Both men continued their routine of attending to ropes, pots and bait. It was Ryan's role to separate usable bait from their catch each day and now he opened the freezer and loaded the bait into the pots. It was a stinking job and Ryan often wondered how he'd been allocated this task while Michael had the easy job of driving the boat out to the reef each day. While he'd quietly accepted the role Michael had assigned him, he didn't like it. He supposed being the elder sibling gave Michael self-appointed rights and his haughty nature made Ryan squirm as both men looked away from each other.

Michael cracked a joke at Jodie's expense and Ryan laughed, weakly – Michael's sense of humour was usually based on other people's misfortune, often at Ryan's expense, and he tried not to dwell on this aspect of his brother's personality – Michael had other traits that Ryan fully endorsed: he was super nice to their parents and now their mother was ill, Michael had set up numerous opportunities for family functions. He was a natural leader, full of talk about the future, and he was easy to communicate with; he stopped to talk to the homeless and he cared about the less fortunate people in the world. So Ryan accepted the good bits and tolerated the bad bits. He likened Michael to a rose bush – capable of producing a beautiful flower but one needed to be mindful of the thorns. Most times, Michael looked and smelt angelic, making it easy to accept his foibles.

***

Hours later, the pots all dropped at a favourite location, Michael clambered down from the boat onto the jetty. 'Hey, Garry! … good to see you,' he yelled.

His uncle looked around and smiled. 'How's the fishing going?' he replied, recognising his nephew.

'We'll know when we pull the pots,' Michael grinned.

Garry's oversized hat sat low on his head, above his usual work gear of drill pants and the 'Boat Lifts and Jetties' polo shirt.

'Would be much better if the government lifted the ban on shark fishing. Flake's in great demand, but we can't bloody deliver! And there's millions of them out there,' Michael added.

The two men walked towards each other as the sun shone in the early autumn afternoon. Soon, they could talk without shouting. 'Well, you'd better make sure you don't fall overboard, young man.'

'Totes,' replied Michael. 'How about you? Are those blokes on the canals paying for their boat docks? And, on an entirely different matter, how's Mum? Have you guys spoken to her lately?'

'Yeah. Donna spoke with her last night and she'll be in town for treatment next week. I'll let you know what days but I'm sure you'll be talking to her before then. What a bummer, eh? So sorry to hear it. Cancer and there's nothing they can do. Make the most of your life while things are still good, young'un.'

Michael watched as his uncle walked towards the work boat he used while installing the floating docks and performing maintenance on private jetties. He stopped to talk to Neil, the barge operator and pile driver. The two old seadogs were good friends and chatted amicably as Michael walked towards his car. Garry often needed to employ staff so frequently they contacted each other to fulfil needs for their mutual benefit, and there were always men of all ages hanging around the docks looking for casual work. It was a symbiotic relationship that suited them both.

As Michael strode along, he wondered why it was his job to find crew and why Ryan couldn't come up with some good ideas. *Clearly, if Jodie's going to be a pain in the neck, Ryan's going to be even more needy. Oh well,* he thought, *that's how life goes at times, I suppose. I guess I'm just glad I don't have a wife. But Mum doesn't need this in her life right now; she has enough to deal with …* The thought made him angry. *Ryan's problems shouldn't be inflicted on our parents.*

With his car in sight, Michael tilted his head upwards to feel the wind direction and predict the weather as he prepared for the days ahead. He could smell the leaves of the trees that grew near the marina and detected the smell of a fire in the distance. It was an autumn smell of leaves falling and trees preparing for the cold days ahead. Hibernation was a good idea, Michael thought, as he crunched dry leaves with each step. Luckily for them, sea creatures didn't hibernate, but inclement weather would limit their catches. Changes in government policies were on the horizon, too, he remembered, and these would create difficulties in the industry; politicians were making decisions they claimed were in the best interests of fishing populations for the future. Yet some species were protected despite evidence of increasing numbers. And then there were the political decisions that affected export contracts as some countries restricted imports.

Then his mind flicked to Jodie, and he remembered the look on her face as she sat in the truck, travelling along without a care in the world. *Where was she going and what was she doing with the truckie?* He decided to befriend the driver and keep an eye on her, knowing she had questionable standards, and once again Michael appreciated his single marital status. *Poor Ryan, having to put up with her.* Then he thought of his mother's attachment to Ryan's daughter, Emily. *Such a sweet kid. A surprise really, considering Jodie is her mother! If Jodie separates from*

Ryan, Mum will be devastated. She loves Emily so much, and then there will be the impact on Ryan which might impact on our fishing partnership. Fear crept over him. *What if she can lay claim to a share of the boat ...* He felt as though someone had walked over his grave.

He shuddered as he reached his car. *That is something we need to deal with soon ... get ahead of her on that one.* He tried to push the dark thoughts away, focused on the rump steak in his fridge just waiting to be barbequed. His mouth started watering as the engine ticked over and the car kicked into gear.

Chapter 6

Fay's Actions

Donna looked forward to seeing Jane but clearly wished it was under different circumstances. So much had changed since Christmas, including her sister becoming terminally ill. She admired Jane's stoicism but knew that, beneath the brave façade, Jane was depressed and upset. Of course, she was! At sixty-eight years of age, she had a right to believe she'd been robbed and dealt an evil hand. She'd suspected for some time something was wrong. Jane's persistent cough and unreasonable tiredness were key indicators, and she knew Jane had sensed the same. Donna shook her head. Of the many people she knew, she could think of no one who deserved to live more than Jane.

Donna thought of the new group of patients she met each year while working night shift at the hospital; she figured close to a hundred and fifty per year. Some were badly behaved, the drug-affected mostly, which often led to criminal activities. She'd become adept at spotting who would be tempted to act up or demand more drugs. Regularly she saw former patients in the shopping centre, and often spoke to them. Donna liked the idea her patients thought she was a fair and trustworthy nurse – that she wasn't too bad as far as someone in authority went.

Her role as a nurse was never far from her thoughts and even as she made up a bed for Jane and Bill for the weekend and thought about Sunday lunch with the family and friends, she reflected on the day's work and what she would need to do next. No day was ever the same at the hospital and Donna liked the unpredictable nature of her job. While others in the game moaned about workloads and patient behaviour, she resigned herself to thinking it was merely a profession and she'd do it to the best of her ability.

'Are we still having lunch here on Sunday?' Garry asked as he emerged from his office after placing an order for another shipping container of dock and jetty components. He raked a hand through his hair as he ambled towards the kitchen to begin preparing the evening meal. Without receiving an answer from Donna, he began peeling potatoes and carrots, whistling as he worked. He liked the domestic harmony in his house, something he knew that was missing in Ryan's house, just a few streets away.

***

Indeed, just a few streets away …

Jodie waited for Ryan to pull into the driveway, shut the car door and step up the concrete steps to the front verandah. She knew Michael had seen her with Andy in the truck. He had deliberately turned and watched her being driven away, and she fumed that he had probably told Ryan. This would thwart her intention of pleading the injured party in her divorce so she needed a plan to override it. *Simply deny it,* she'd decided. *Heaven knows there are millions of girls with long blonde hair who looked just like me, who would take a ride with a truckie. Next time,* she reminded herself, *keep your voice down to avoid being identified. You need to fly under the radar for however long it takes for divorce proceedings to start. And that needs to start asap. So I have to get Ryan to pack his things and move out so I can claim the house.*

Jodie began moving about the kitchen without talking, waiting for him to ask about Andy when she took her chance that Michael hadn't said anything. The tension in the air was palpable, both waiting for the arguments to start, knowing the prolonged silence between them was heading to the day's explosion. Jodie, her back to him as she sliced carrots at the sink, lit the wick.

'Ryan, I can't keep doing this. You can keep living here for a short while, but ultimately, you have to move out. Emily shouldn't be exposed to all our arguments.'

Ryan's jaw dropped open. 'Wha …? What?! Don't keep pushing this, Jodie. You are the one who keeps starting arguments! You seem to have it all worked out before I walk in the door.'

She turned to face him, her teeth gritted. He could see the hatred in her eyes. 'You are pretty dumb if you can't see our relationship's not working.'

'Marriage, Jodie. It's called a marriage.'

'Whatever,' she quipped. 'I have been unhappy for a very long time and can't keep doing this. You have to go. Emily, of course, will stay here as this is her home and I'm her mother.'

'You are not taking Emily away from me … don't even think it.' His first thought was to hurl her out the back door, but that would only give her ammunition, and a reason to have him removed from the house, so instead, he quickened his steps to the bathroom, deliberately ignoring her next words. He didn't need any more fuel on the fire. Noisily, he splashed water around to wash his face and hands, prolonging this activity for as long as he could before going out into the kitchen to face more words intended to cause an eruption. Emily now sat at the kitchen table drawing letters and practising her numbers – his beautiful little Emily. So he stayed silent. He wouldn't argue in front of Emily though he felt sure his silence strengthened the tension in the room. He just wasn't going to play into Jodie's hands, with the domestic abuse line, and disagreeing with her would upset his daughter. Normally, he would have reached into the fridge for a beer, but this time he overtly took a glass from the cupboard and filled it with water. He added some cordial to ensure it was seen as a beverage of enjoyment, and from now on, he would refrain from having alcohol in the house. He didn't want any evidence to fuel her accusation of him being a heavy drinker on the agenda.

Ryan knew he had to play the game too. If he left the house, he was a deserter. If he had a beer, he was a drunkard. If he argued with his wife or even presented a different point of view, he was an abuser. He felt snookered!

Later that evening, when Emily was fast asleep, Ryan looked at Jodie as she sat reading in front of the television. 'Did you go to work today?'

'I had some business to attend to,' she replied cagily. Clearly, she wasn't going to divulge her whereabouts to him. She kept reading.

Jodie's jaw set as she tried to stay focused on the page, but Ryan's stern gaze in her peripheral vision unnerved her. She had fully intended to stay overnight at Andy's place, and now, with Ryan feeling so wounded, she could rely on him being home at night to look after Emily and, if need be, take her to school in the mornings. Indeed, regardless of what Michael told Ryan, she had every intention of seeing more of Andy.

Remembering their previous interlude at his place made her smile. She definitely wanted this new man in her life, and he would be if she had anything to do with it. A new love interest was just what she needed. If she had to wait twelve months after she got him out of the house, Andy might not stick around that long. Therefore, she had to force the issue and get

Ryan forcibly removed. But right now, she needed to start an argument so she could storm out of the house and go to Andy's.

***

A week later, Jane had more business to attend to with Stan, who had notified her of the arrival of the second large sum of cash she'd requested from her account. She took possession of the two large envelopes of cash, and accepted Stan's security escort out to her car, all the while expressing his surprise that Bill had not come to help her home safely with such a large amount.

'It's a surprise,' she reminded him with a smile. 'There's going to be some happiness back in our house soon,' she continued the ruse.

At home, she placed the envelopes with the others in her safe place, hiding the money away from Bill's sight. After his initial reaction to her intention, she had wisely not involved him in any way to avoid any kind of recrimination after her passing. She would suggest to him later about giving the boys some cash to tide them over, maybe in the next few months when he would have forgotten her comment about a 'hit'. Then she reconsidered. Bill would want to be present when she handed the money to them, part of the celebration that just wasn't going to happen. Not until she was gone, anyway. She just prayed Stan remained quiet about her withdrawals and her 'surprise'.

She needed now to act with haste and engage in her eradication of Jodie while she was still well enough to function. She could feel in her bones she would soon be bedridden or unable to carry through on her task.

The speedway event that had been held in the town annually was fast approaching; it always enticed a number of people who looked like they'd do anything for their next hit. Sometimes they would linger around town long after the smell of high-octane fuel and burning rubber had dissipated, looking like the kind you would cross the road to avoid. She'd even seen some suspect activity in town, like the passing of cash and small containers ... *or have I been watching too many crime shows on TV these days? Mind, I'm not stupid,* she mused. She just had to get Bill to take her to the speedway – something she had always avoided in the past.

***

A fortnight later, when Jane was hanging out her washing, she heard the side gate click and she looked around to see Fay bustling along the path.

'Hello, Jane! I brought some cake for morning tea,' her friend called out.

Jane's pulse quickened. The next part of her plan was ready to implement. She let the washing drop back into the basket and gave Fay a hug.

'Come on in. I'm trying to get this washing done before the rain comes.' Actually, it was starting to become an effort for her to lift heavy loads and Fay could see it.

'Let me take that,' she said. 'Now you go and make the tea and I'll finish hanging these out.'

Jane relinquished the basket. 'Once I would have said it can wait, that I have all the time in the world to do it, but not anymore.'

'Go on,' Fay half-smiled. 'Go make us some tea. That you do have time for.'

The flywire door slammed shut as Fay made her way into the kitchen where Jane was pouring water into cups. Fay looked around and was pleasantly surprised that the kitchen hadn't changed. She worried at times that a decline in Jane's health may well be characterised by signs of neglect in her home. And Jane would hate that. Her Yucca plant sat on the coffee table with magazines spread around it showing evidence of recent reading. Breakfast dishes were spread across the sink but there was no sign of last night's dinner plates or pots. Fay nodded inwardly. Order still reigned. But for how long was the question. They lived in the country, but Jane would need more regular care and treatment soon and there was a lot of uncertainty about the next few months. Today was good that she'd been invited for morning tea.

The clattering of cups being brought to the table set the mood for a quiet, cosy chat. Fay's eyes rested on the empty cat bowl in the corner of the room. So, Jane and Bill were good at assuming normality. She remembered back to when they'd acquired a cat, the stray having wandered in one cold, wet night and generous Bill had given it food. From that moment on, the cat had found a new and caring home – it was how Bill and Jane functioned. When a creature needed help, it received help.

Her hand trembled as she took a sheet of paper from her handbag and reluctantly put it on the table. 'A phone number, Jane.' Fay released her hand from the paper and took a sip from her tea. *There it was: the details Jane needed.* For a moment, Fay felt Jane was oblivious to the information as she focused on cutting a piece of cake. She held the knife firmly in her hand, almost spiritually, as she let it slide through the fully laden, leftover Christmas cake. Neither woman was religious, but Jane let her mind drift to the Last Supper in the Geseminy

Garden, wondering how Jesus felt as he faced a certain cruel death. If going against her better judgement and principles would help her friend through this, then she would do this.

Quickly Jane jerked herself back to the present. 'I'm surprised I still have some cake. Somehow, we've lost our appetites in recent weeks.'

'Jane, it's hardly surprising. How are Michael and Ryan taking the news? Silly question. I'm sure they're devastated. And poor little Emily too.'

'I don't think Ryan and Jodie have told Emily. At eight, perhaps she's too young to understand. After all, how old does one need to be to understand death? I hope they don't say anything to her really. I guess the boys take it in their stride. They don't say much. Bill's the one who is thinking too much. The other day I watched him boil the kettle at least three or four times before he poured the water. I guess he's just in his own world, merely thinking and trying to be normal. Sometimes, I catch him staring into space. When he sees me, he pretends to do something.'

Fay held her cup with both hands as she lifted it to her mouth. 'I guess each person digests it in their own way. Do you try to keep busy?'

'When I find myself with morbid thoughts, I walk around the block or go for a drive. I focus on the garden and just think about putting one foot in front of the other. The therapist suggested physical exercise as a coping mechanism, and I think it works as effectively as anything. I try not to think of the past or the future, too, as it makes me teary. Sometimes, though, I just have a good old bawl, though I try not to let Bill see me.'

Fay shifted uncomfortably in her seat as she felt herself tear up. Then each woman sat in their own private hell, not knowing what to say or do, except look at the table or the floor. Finally, Jane took the piece of paper and put it in a drawer near the sink. 'Thank you, Fay. I just appreciate it so much. Clearly, we'll keep this strictly between ourselves. That's important. So you are all set with what you need now?'

Jane almost nodded. 'I've just got to convince Bill to take me to the speedway so …'

Fay had that covered. 'You can come with us. John does a great job for the Lion's Club, managing the venue and keeping all those drop-kicks under control. Some are not too bad, but some are really bad types and he has to keep a close eye on them. I hope you can cope with the noise and exhaust fumes. And be prepared … it tears up the showgrounds, but is good economically for the town. That's the reason they hold it here.' She paused for a moment. 'It's all in your hands now, Jane, and I won't mention this again. The less said, the better.'

The two friends hugged, and Fay made her way towards the flywire door which marked the end of her visit.

Chapter 7

Jane's Preparations

Donna scanned the shopping list as she thought about the family lunch on Sunday. With cooler weather sneaking in through the front door, she decided to cook a pot of soup, and a chicken curry – Jane's favourite. She would also need to think about preparing Jane's room, though she hadn't even asked her yet about palliative care. She physically squirmed as she thought of ideas around palliative care, but this term hadn't been discussed. Jane's visits to the hospital had become more frequent, which would be natural as her sister fought against her illness. Meanwhile, she would wait until Jane referred to it in conversation.

***

For Jane, at her home in Carinya, palliative care was the furthest thing from her mind, though she knew she could run out of time if she didn't make some kind of progress on her plan. *How dare that girl state she is tired of my son, and simply discards him. How dare she try and rob him of all he has worked for. And she thinks she'll have the law on her side by using Emily! You'll never get the …*

She quickly dismissed these thoughts; she needed a clear head for what she had to do next, and as she headed for her car, she checked her bag to ensure the all-important piece of paper lay within it. Assured it was, she headed off. Her instructions on Fay's sheet of paper were abundantly clear: call the number from a public phone box well away from your location. That way the call could not be traced back. So Jane drove the long distance to Port Burnie where she knew there was a public phone box and she made the call to arrange a meeting.

Her fingers shook as she entered the number, and jumped when a deep, gruff voice on the other end answered. He said one word, 'Speak.'

'I've been given your number for a service which I will discuss with you if you are interested,' Jane read from the note she had written out, speaking it word for word as she'd written it. She knew she'd be too distressed to articulate her need concisely to a stranger – a thug, no less! Her legs felt like jelly; the muscles in her stomach worked overtime, making her nauseous. My name is …'

'No names, lady. I don't get yours, you don't get mine. How did you get this number?'

Jane's voice almost left her. 'A … a friend … she knows I need something done.'

'Something done. Not something … you need something *done.*'

'Y … yes.' Jane's heart rate quickened.

'If I've got the gist right,' the voice said, 'temporary or permanent.'

Jane's heartbeat pounded in her ears till she could hardly hear. 'Permanent,' she said meekly.

'You sound like someone's grandma, lady,' he said, almost with a laugh.

Suddenly bravado struck Jane's psyche. 'Maybe I am, young man,' she said firmly. 'But I am serious.' Her knees started to shake again.

'Who?' he said. 'No names.'

'Family member,' Jane said bluntly, starting to fall into a crime TV show negotiation scene she'd seen. This seemed to run just like the show, Bill puzzled why she'd suddenly taken to watching true crime documentaries. She couldn't get enough of them.

'What do you expect to gain out of this?' he queried next.

Jane felt suddenly cold. *Can I really go through with this?* 'My son's freedom,' she said meekly again.

'Okay.' The man paused for a long moment. 'Give me the number of that phone box. We'll ring back in one hour. Be there to take the call.'

'Oh … alright,' Jane almost whispered.

She sat in the car for nearly an hour, then returned to the phone box. The phone rang dead on the hour. It was a different voice this time. She thought it sounded familiar. He ascertained that she wanted something done.

Jane said, 'Yes.'

'I hope you're cashed up …'

Jane remained silent, hoping she had enough.

'It'll cost you twenty … big ones.'

An episode of True Crime flicked through her mind, and she suddenly realised the element she was dealing with. How could she be sure they would do it once she paid them. There were insurances, she remembered from one TV show. 'Half before and half after,' she said, trying to sound like she knew what she was doing.

'Deal.'

Jane's eyes narrowed as she tried to conjure up a face that went with the voice. She was sure she had heard that voice before. 'How do we do this?' she asked, not sure how the rest of her plan would play out.

'When?' he posed the next question.

'That depends on how soon you want your money.' *That sounds really professional,* Jane thought, getting right into the role she had seen on TV. 'I will leave it up to you. Just don't leave it too long.' Jane had already told Ryan to stand firm and not move out of the house. As long as he stood firm on that, time could be random. If it became too difficult for him, then it needed to be sooner. She just hoped he was strong enough to deal with the daily arguments.

'We'll do the first payment exchange well out of the way … at a little town called Carinya. There'll be a speedway on there in a couple of weeks so a good reason for you to be there. There's a park in the centre of town, with a tree that has a hollow in the trunk. You can't miss it. On the morning of the speedway, put the cash in an envelope with a photo of the target and where they can be located in that hollow.'

Jane was still racking her brain for an image of the speaker. *God, I know that voice. I'm tempted to say, I know you …* but voices rang out, warning her not to do so.

'Two months later to the day, deposit the final payment in the same place. You got that?'

Jane nodded, then remembered to say, 'Yes.'

'Thank you for your business.' And the call disconnected.

My God. Carinya! I am supposed to do this far from home, but it is on my bloody doorstep. For a moment she considered backing out of it. She wasn't any murderer. Surely, there was another way of dealing with Jodie … Maybe all she had to do was not leave the money in the park, and nothing would happen. Maybe she should dwell on it a while longer … see how Ryan would sort it out.

Slowly she returned to her car, still considering. Then she put the car into gear and headed back to Carinya, counting to a hundred backwards to steel her racing heart beat, just like her psychologist had told her.

'Ah, there you are!' Bill called from the office as she entered the house through the heavy front door. 'I was wondering where you were. Donna rang confirming lunch arrangements for Sunday. She doesn't want you to bring anything and has offered us a bed for the weekend.'

Jane was astounded – to think normality could just wander through the door and seep into their home. 'Oh good. You've put the veggies on. Bit early to cook the steak but it's defrosting in the fridge when you're ready.'

She kicked off her shoes and placed her handbag on the bench. 'Did the plumber come to install the water heating unit?'

Bill murmured something from the office, which Jane assumed was an affirmation, otherwise he would be ranting about workmen not doing jobs properly. 'Apparently, all the gang will be there, including the boys. Not sure about Jodie, but who cares about her anyway. Let's hope we see Emily. Good to see Michael and Ryan working so well together on the boat.'

When Bill joined Jane in the kitchen, she was not surprised to see him showered and dressed in his tracksuit ready to watch the News on TV. Bill was dependable, though impatient at times, but with Jane's new knowledge, she looked at him and smiled.

'What?' he asked.

'Nothing. I've just had quite a good day really. And now, with Donna and Garry's for the weekend, I think my life is on track.' She looked away to ensure she wouldn't raise any suspicions as her life, with chemo ahead, was anything but rosy. She wasn't sure how much chemo she'd have and there would be many conversations with doctors soon.

She poured a glass of wine and sat down in the comfy lounge chair to watch television. As she allowed her eyelids to drop, it was like pulling down a blind, and she felt relieved the situation had been instigated and now, if she made the payment, it would be totally out of her control. The man's familiar voice still rattled around in her head.

She closed her eyes, feeling drained. She could cheerfully sleep forever right now, then she jolted upright, realising she needed to stay alive until the deed was done, and she had made the final payment. She was on a time frame! *Six weeks – two to the speedway and one month thereafter.* She took a sip of her wine, mentally raising the glass and saying *This one is for Ryan.*

'I'll start cooking the meat outside now,' Bill said, looking inside the fridge.

Jane eyes closed again, tired from the long drive there and back, and she realised she wasn't far off sleep. The television droned on and on, describing some world catastrophe but now she was impervious to any news at all. She remained in her chair and let the wine slide down her throat. She briefly considered Bill might check the car speedo and ask her where her long drive had taken her. He was quite particular about details with the car. But, she decided, she was quite entitled to merely drive around aimlessly now she had a terminal illness. She almost laughed aloud but restrained herself as Bill let the back door slam behind him. She decided to take a walk later in the evening so Bill wouldn't press her for information pertaining to the afternoon events. She didn't want to lie, and she needed to clear her head. It would help her sleep now she had a plan in place. Gone was uncertainty and the instructions ahead were very clear. She thought about her next move and realised all she had to do was wait but, for what, she wasn't sure. Then the thought crossed her mind: *these thugs are aware of what they need to know. I'm sure I'll be told somehow about Jodie's absence. From what Ryan has hinted, Jodie is already absent a few nights here and there. Of course, she was!* Jane felt sure Ryan knew where she was going but wasn't saying. He probably even knew the name of her new lover. *Maybe a conversation with Emily will reveal much about her mother.* However, Jane realised how little Emily cared about details. Her role in all this had been done and would soon be paid for. For now, she just needed to have the money ready and keep it safe, and find a reasonable photo of Jodie. She suppressed a smile, and reminded herself forcefully to stay alive in the interim.

Dinner was served!

Chapter 8

Sunday Lunch

Bill's mouth watered at the smell of cooking meat wafting throughout the house as he made his way through the front door. Roast lamb was one of his favourites, though Jane rarely cooked it these days. She used to love making meals and cooking cakes, but recently, he'd noticed she only baked when it was necessary. For now, though, Bill luxuriated in anticipation of juicy meat and baked vegetables, all drowned in thick gravy. His nostrils were in overdrive!

'Hello, Donna,' he called as he strode into the hallway and towards the kitchen, which was crowded with people he knew and loved. Family gatherings were his favourite activity these days, particularly when good hearty food was involved.

An assortment of plates and dishes were spread all over the bench, and chatter filled the air around him. Bill's phone vibrated in his pocket and he pulled it out, checking the caller identification as he did. It was Garry.

'What are you doing ringing me? There's a party at your place.' He stepped outside into the laundry for some privacy. 'What's up?'

'Look, I'm just at the marina and I'll be home soon. I had to meet Neil, the pile driver.'

'On a Sunday?'

'This was his only free day – you know what it's like in business ... when the job calls, we're there. Hmm, actually I was hoping to have a chat now so I can talk in private without all the noise of everyone. Bill, do you want work at any time? Perhaps a day or two? Or more? Just like your boys, I'm having trouble getting staff. Do you still have a current truck licence? Better still a semi?'

'A truck licence, yes. A semi licence, no. It's been a while since I've driven one so I might need a refresher at my age.' Silently Bill gathered his thoughts. 'The short answer to your question is after a few months I can probably drive a truck for you, but not while Jane needs me.' Bill realised his ruthlessness in his response to Garry, but he quickly remembered doctors' conversations about Jane's illness. With winter on their doorstep, he'd been told Jane would not see Christmas. He hoped, of course, that she had more time but her indifference about treatment meant her future was travelling along a path medicine couldn't predict. She would grow weaker and her pain would increase, signalling the need for more intensive pain management, and that would make her sleep more.

Bill ended his phone conversation and, with a trembling hand, put his phone in his pocket. As he entered the kitchen, he saw Jane calmly unpacking the esky.

She had followed closely behind Bill but then had moved away from him as she realised he was taking a phone call. The heavy esky was full of food to share with hungry folk, who now spilled through the house and into the backyard. Chairs dotted around the garden and decking, and glasses, drinks and food graced a long table. Jane helped Bill with the esky as food magically appeared on the bench top, ready for eating. She followed him out through the doors, taking a moment to scan familiar, happy faces as she was guided to a comfortable chair, which she took without question as tiredness began to overtake her. Sinking deep into the fabric, she sighed with relief.

Bill brought her some orange juice and then quickly scanned the guests so he could plan his conversation. But all too quickly, Michael was by his side, which made Bill smile as his son sidled up to him.

'Hi, Dad,' his son said as he put a can of beer into his hand. 'Mum's looking good.'

Bill wasn't sure if it was a statement or a question. 'She is now but take note of how much she moves around today. My bet is she'll be sitting in that chair, and others will come and chat with her. I cannot see her helping with food today. Anyway, Donna'll have it all organised. But your mother? … Yep, she's doing well.'

A comfortable silence lingered between them as they tried to watch Jane without being noticed.

'Why doesn't she accept more chemo treatment?' Michael said critically.

'I think she knows the outcome will be inevitable. Perhaps she doesn't want to linger. Do you know we actually haven't discussed it, but recently she's been distant, but I've just put it down to depression. Who knows? I've noticed she spends time going for long walks and long drives too. I don't question her as it sounds like an inquisition.' He half-shrugged. 'I try to distract her with other things.'

'But don't you go with her?' Michael asked, almost accusingly. His eyes levelled with his father's.

'Sometimes, particularly when she walks around the block or simply down the street. A bit strange but I have noticed she just takes off in the car. Perhaps she hasn't got the strength to walk. I'm not sure. Soon enough, she'll lose her independence, and I'll have to accompany her. I figure she just likes some time alone. But this won't last. Doctors don't really say much.'

Bill looked at the table hoping some of the cooked meat would appear, as the aroma still lingered in his nostrils. He was hungry, and it had been some time since he and Jane had eaten breakfast.

'Perhaps they don't know. When the cancer metastasises, things will become even more uncertain. For now, we just take each day as it comes.' Bill's back began to ache and he knew he'd been standing for too long; he looked around for a seat or a bench where he could rest his aching body. He noticed Ryan sitting at another table, so he excused himself on the pretence of finding a chair.

'You've got a crook back, Dad?' Ryan kept eating potato chips from the bowl as he spoke. Somewhere in the background, a noisy crow cawed, signalling its desire to join the party. Other tiny birds hopped about more discretely, waiting patiently in silence for a crumb to drop on a path or in the garden so they could unceremoniously peck it up.

'Oh, you know how these aches and pains set in. But then again, thankfully, you don't.'

The two men paused in easy silence as guests mingled seamlessly in Donna and Garry's backyard. Bill sensed pain in his youngest son and leaned in closer as he spoke quietly, 'You all right, son?' He tried to smile.

'Dunno know, Dad. I think Michael is thinking of selling the boat. We seem to have trouble getting a crew and, honestly, some blokes are just so unreliable. And Mike seems to get irritable and short-tempered easily these days. Recently, I asked him how things were, but he just got in a huff and walked off.'

Ryan looked away, annoyed that he'd said anything. He didn't want to worry his father about business when there were lots of other issues at stake. For a moment it seemed like his father hadn't heard him. His dad had been an easy-going man when he and Michael were growing up, but he was dealing with a lot right now, so he didn't want to add to his woes. 'Perhaps now the season's coming to an end, he's had some time to think', Ryan continued. 'He probably doesn't want to do winter maintenance where the money seems to flow outwards at a rate of knots. Just lifting the boat and putting it on the slipway for antifouling costs a fortune, and each year, it continues to increase. Repair this, replace that. I don't know! I'll just let things chill for a bit and ask him later if he still seems unsettled. But I think it's getting blokes to crew each day that's a problem.'

Ryan frowned and took a mouthful of beer, using it as a distraction. Right now, he had other factors to consider but he wasn't going to give voice to his marriage problems. He'd stay like an ostrich with its head in the sand so if he didn't say anything, then the situation didn't exist. But he knew it did.

His thoughts shifted to Jodie and her indifference to their problems. He'd recently seen her in a truck with a man and was pleased when Mike told him he'd check out the number plate to identify who Jodie was spending her time with. They had both seen seagulls picking live fish from the back of the truck, indicating Jodie's friend was in too much of a hurry to tarp his load. This being a reportable offence, they decided to do so to get back at him. Besides, the driver wasn't looking after the interests of the fishermen and the industry. And reporting him would give them reason to check out the driver more closely. Ryan wondered if this relationship was just a fling, or was it something more serious.

The thought of Jodie's flippant laughter made his stomach churn. He was glad, in a way, that she hadn't wanted to come today – she and Emily had planned to see a movie. He'd thought that rather strange, but was happy Emily seemed contented and occupied, even though she was missing associating with her grandmother. For now, the situation was a day-by-day saga and Ryan felt like he was constantly waiting for something to happen. He diverted his focus; heard his dad say quietly to Garry:

'Look, I think we should sell our place and buy something in Port Burnie. With Jane so ill, we'll need to be close to medical services, and I don't want to live in Carinya alone. I've been thinking about it for a while, but I haven't discussed it with Jane yet. I don't think she'll like the idea. Apart from Carinya being her home, it'll signal her demise and, ultimately, what her future holds. Anyway, let's see what the winter brings and wait until we can buy a house near you or the boys.'

Garry nodded that it was a good idea.

***

One day, several weeks later, something *did* happen, yet Ryan realised it was more about what didn't happen …

He'd pulled his ute slowly into the driveway, as usual; alighted from the cab and walked nonchalantly up the path towards the clothesline and back door, where he slipped off his boots and let his smelly overalls drop around his ankles onto the back verandah. He shut the door quietly to keep out the autumn chill as he glanced at young Emily doing her homework at the kitchen table.

'Hello, Cutie,' he'd said, as he had countless times, and moved towards the table to see what she was writing. 'Mum home?'

'No. She left a note to say she was out shopping and wouldn't be home until tomorrow.'

Ryan turned his head to read the note and then smelt dinner cooking. The table had been set for two so at least there was no hostility at this stage of the day, he considered. He didn't know where Jodie would be and knew if he called her, it would go to voice mail. This had become a pattern in recent weeks —

63

months – when he thought about it. As usual, he felt unsettled but tried to put on a brave face for Emily as he opened the oven door to see a roast dinner cooking and savour the delicious smells. *She can't have been gone that long ...*

He let the hot water run over him in the shower and turned his thoughts to the day on the boat. Now he was home, he would make some phone calls to organise a crew for the next few days, thus pacifying Mike by sharing the load. They'd had a good season to date and had managed to cut their costs by catching a few sharks to keep the bait cost down. It was totally illegal, of course, *but, such is the life of a fisherman.* Remembering the price of the recent gas bill, he turned off the revitalising warm water and stepped out of the steamy shower.

***

The next morning, Jodie hadn't come home, so Ryan left her a note as he prepared to take Emily to school. This routine suited them both, and they enjoyed a leisurely breakfast together. The kettle was boiling happily, and toast was jumping up from the toaster, eager to be eaten while warm.

'I love the cool weather now,' Emily blurted out. 'Soon it'll be raining, and I can wear my raincoat.'

Ryan also liked the cooler weather as it meant fewer early morning fishing runs and a rather less hectic pace in his life. 'Make sure your lunch is packed,' he called out as he donned his fishing clothes, ready to make his way to the marina.

Slowly, the ute left the driveway, with the occupants totally unaware of the chaos and hell that would soon break loose.

Chapter 9

The Dilemma

Tiredness swept over Bill as he loaded luggage into the car boot for the trip from Port Burnie to Carinya. He hadn't slept well the previous night as snippets of conversations from the family lunch disturbed him, causing him to toss and turn all night in Garry and Donna's spare room. Jane had slept soundly, thankfully, and Bill had been relieved to hear the regular deep breathing of someone relaxed and resting. He couldn't stop thinking about his suggestion of selling their home in Carinya and moving to Port Burnie. It was a great idea and one that had been simmering away but now that he had verbalised the notion, it had developed legs and grown overnight. He decided to discuss it with Jane on the way home, and did.

'Jane, I've been thinking,' Bill started soon after they'd left town. 'How about we move house to be closer to the family?' He braced himself to hear all sorts of protests, but the quietness between them surprised him. The seconds roared on. The engine continued to drone in his ears. Bill forced himself to silence – he'd made his statement –asked the question. Now an answer had to be forthcoming.

'Actually, I've been thinking the same thing,' Jane finally said. 'I know my heart belongs in Carinya, but it might just make life easier on many different fronts.'

Bill's hands relaxed on the steering wheel, the tension that had built up from expecting Jane's resistance immediately dissipating. He'd forgotten how rational she was, and he glanced at her as he drove and smiled. He remembered how easy she was to live with, and his heart contracted as he remembered the first time they'd met. He'd simply loved the way she looked, and as he grew to know her, he soon felt he couldn't live without her. It was love, he reasoned! And he'd refused to consider life without her. Right now, they were living each day as it came, knowing change was on its way and this change was not welcome.

Their neighbour Ned was outside mowing his lawn when Bill and Jane arrived home. Ned stopped the engine and leant over his fence. 'Looks like rain, so I thought I'd better prepare for some cold weather coming.'

'No work today?'

'No. I worked a double shift on the weekend. Big brawl at the pub so they called for backup. I didn't get to bed until midnight so at least it gives me time off now. That's one good thing about a country copper's job. One never knows when there's going to be a drama somewhere or an accident on the road.'

Jane liked the safety of living next to a policeman, even if Fay did consider him slimy. Now, when they were considering moving to Port Burnie, she wouldn't know her neighbours. A lump grew in her throat as she realised it wouldn't really matter as she wasn't going to live much longer. She sat in the car as Bill unpacked the bags and took them into the house; felt the tears roll down her cheeks as she looked towards Ned and Lola's house with the smoke coming out of the chimney. Their lounge room would be warm and cosy, she knew it so well. Of course, she didn't really want to move but her head told her it was necessary.

Eventually, she opened the car door, stepped out onto the path, and walked slowly into the house, her breathing shallow with the effort. She had only enough energy to sink into the chair as exhaustion suddenly hit her. Her eyes shut, and she soon drifted off to sleep despite the daylight coming in through the window. The ringing of the phone woke her.

'Hi Jane! You arrived home okay? Wasn't it a great day yesterday seeing everyone here? We'll get together again soon, but don't forget you can stay here if you like when you're having medical treatment.'

'Donna, I won't be having any more chemo or surgery. There's no point with this being so aggressive and it makes me feel so ill … so useless. I already have good and not-so-good days, which the oncologist tells me is normal, but I just want good days, Donna, for as long as I can. Peg wants me to liaise with the oncologist from now on, so I'm going to do this my way. I'll be all right until the cancer metastasises. Then palliative care will start.'

And that was what happened. Jane came off chemotherapy.

***

Bill and Jane had many plans to make before the idea of selling and moving house became public knowledge. The mindlessness of television was a source of comfort as they sat and watched movement on a screen before going to bed. And that was all it was, movement.

As they enjoyed their morning coffee, Bill took out the newspaper and opened to the Real Estate section. It meant the beginning of the end for Jane, but she knew she needed to endorse this idea of moving into a large town with adequate medical facilities. She tried to look interested but her attention was limited. She struggled and Bill could see this.

'How about I arrange all this business and you merely look after yourself?'

A mix of emotions swept over her as she agreed to Bill's proposal. In her own mind, other things took precedence. She had already deposited the first payment into the tree truck before the speedway meeting and had sat there through the infernal noise, eyeing the low types that lurked around the showgrounds. One of them would have collected the money. And one of them was going to do something despicable that would save her family and keep it together. She still had two long brown envelopes to deposit in the tree – she just wondered now how she would know the job had been done before she did that.

Later that week, the phone rang. It was Ryan.

Without any small talk about his mother's health, he said, 'Mum, do you think you and Dad could come down and stay with us a while? I'm not sure what's happening with Jodie, but she's gone away for a bit. Not sure where or for how long. I can't contact her. Perhaps you could come sometime next week if she hasn't come home by then? I just need some help getting Emily to school until I can arrange something a bit more permanent.'

The phone went quiet for a moment as Ryan drew breath. 'That bloody Jodie! She does this just when Mike wants to do as many boat runs as possible before the winter rains set in. Once fishing stops, we'll be right. But for now, I'm a bit stuck.'

Jane's jaw dropped open, and her legs felt weaker than usual. She stood speechless. Then Bill arrived and placed a chair for her to sit on, and took the phone from her hand. She told him what Ryan wanted.

'Of course, son,' Bill responded keenly. 'We've got a few things happening here but nothing for you to worry about.

Keep us posted but we'll prepare to be at yours this time next week if nothing's changed.' They rang off.

Jane remained seated, wondering. *Has the situation been taken care of? Jodie's away, but how temporary this is remains to be seen.* Momentarily, Jane felt dreadful. *But why?* she questioned herself. *Why feel dreadful? That was the plan, wasn't it? And now it's unfolding, perhaps.* She now had to stay to the schedule of depositing the last payment, one part of her hoping she was paying for a service, one part of her wishing that nothing had happened. There had to be another way.

***

Ryan hung up the phone and tried to settle the shaking that inhabited his whole being. *How dare Jodie be so irresponsible! It's one thing to stay away for a bit, but now it's ongoing. And now she won't answer her phone.* Indeed, it went to Voicemail every single time! And then it said the phone was out of range or switched off. *Has she really abandoned Emily?*

That first week, he went through the motions of taking Emily to school every day and going on to work from there, usually looking for Jodie along the streets as he drove to meet Mike on the jetty. The air was tense between them as he'd had to abandon his early morning work of pulling the pots in lieu of Emily's school run, so, naturally, Mike wasn't happy. *But it's easy for him … he doesn't have a kid to look after.* He sure needed his parents to help out – or anyone. Jodie's absence had become problematic, and he didn't know how to answer Emily's questions concerning Jodie's whereabouts or who had picked her up, given her car was still in the driveway. All he could do was wait.

***

At nine o'clock one Tuesday morning, with the wind blowing quietly from the east, Jodie had heard a car horn beeping. She'd looked out the window to where a white van had parked in her driveway. The beeping horn had attracted her, calling to her to see what the driver wanted. She'd approached the vehicle, and as she'd arrived at the passenger door, two men appeared from behind the van and grabbed her. She'd screamed, loudly, and writhed against their grip as they yanked open the door and forced her into the van. But there was no one around to hear or see her. The two men pushed her into the back seat and dragged a hood over her head. She heard metallic sounds then felt the cold metal as something encompassed her wrists.

She heard the vehicle roar as it catapulted backwards onto the road and sped away. She struggled on, but all the while strong knees and hands pushed her down.

It had all unfolded so quickly she didn't have time to register what was happening. But she knew to be afraid. *What's happening? Is someone playing a joke?* A thick band of tape was pressed over her mouth, stopping those questions, and she soon realised it wasn't a joke – her life was in danger.

The thick fabric of the hood stank of stale, rancid food that had perished long ago, and the wristbands were incredibly tight and cut into her wrists. The hood was tight around her eyes, so she closed them, seeking comfort. Even if her eyes were open, she couldn't see anything at all. Her world had fallen into darkness. Every time she moved, her bindings cut in deeper but it didn't stop her from screaming and fighting as best she could. Soon her shoulders ached terribly from the unnatural position she'd been forced into with her hands behind her back, and before long, she fell against the seat and realised she couldn't move. Excruciating pain sank in and her tears flowed and soaked into the horrible cloth over her head. She absolutely couldn't move, and though shouting seemed pointless, she didn't stop trying.

As the vehicle roared along the road, Jodie heard the men talking, their voices stern and abrupt, one speaking with a foreign accent. She didn't know how many men were involved—three at least—two in the back with her and one driving.

After what felt like an eternity, the vehicle became more stable, and she assumed they were driving along a straight country road. The men ceased talking and the engine settled into an angry, relentless hum, the tyres seeming to find every bump in the road which increased her pain. All kinds of terrifying thoughts entered her head! *Are these men going to kill me? Why? Why did they take me?*

The bile in her stomach threatened to rise to her throat and she struggled to keep it down. Soon her head began to ache. This continued until she thought she would pass out. As soon as the idea came into her head, she hoped the time would quickly arrive for this to happen. She now battled to breathe as the fabric of the hood stuck to her face, and she couldn't move enough to get the tape away from her mouth so she could breathe better. *Perhaps I'll suffocate*, she thought, and so the struggle to breathe became a terrifying reality. *Jesus*, she thought, *this is my last day on Earth*!

She could feel her face moisten from her crying and trying to breathe; at the same time, her head felt it was going to split. It continued until, at long last, the vehicle slowed.

The engine ground to a halt and the men's voices started up again. The darkness of the hood terrified her. Not knowing what was going to happen equally so. *Are they going to rape me?* She was in so much pain any kind of movement would be a relief. Someone grabbed her arm and dragged her out of the vehicle onto the hard ground. The hood and metal wrist restraints made movement impossible, and struggling only intensified her pain. As she lay on the dirt, she could hear the little ticking noises engines made when they were turned off and cooling. Apart from that, it was silent. No bird noises. No sounds of civilisation even faintly detected. Her skin felt cold. Then she heard shuffling noises. Someone was near her. The only smell she noticed was her body odour wafting around the hood and permeating her nostrils. *Is this what fear smells like?*

Then hands pushed her and rolled her onto what felt like cold plastic; her legs were lifted and thrust into what felt like a large package. She heard a zip doing up – in her panic, it was deafening. Then she realised she was in what she could only imagine was a vinyl sleeping bag, one that totally encased her, head and all … like a body bag. At that, she screamed, but it echoed back in her ears, and she thrashed but to no avail. The hood and metal cuffs remained tight, and nothing she did helped.

Feeling horribly sick, the bile rose again into Jodie's mouth and oozed onto her face. Men's voices, one in that foreign tongue, began speaking again as she realised they were shouting instructions to each other.

Then Jodie felt jostled as the bag was lifted. Roughly, she was carried a short distance and then dropped, starting her pain all over again. She heard the muffled words, 'We come back.'

Then the voices slowly diminished and she assumed they had dumped her and had shuffled away.

After several minutes, the vehicle engine started, roared under acceleration, and then faded as it left. Jodie lay still for long hours, listening, hoping they would return, trying to breathe through the heavy fabric hood, through the heavy plastic cover. Slowly, her eyelids closed against her will and, her head thumping, she lost consciousness. Nothing happened for days. Time turned into weeks. And she didn't escape.

Chapter 10

The Final Payment

Jane waited and waited. Soon she and Bill would be going to stay at Ryan's to help out in Jodie's absence. *But is she really missing or just spending time away from Ryan?* she pondered, a cold sweat rising on her face as she rose from the garden chair where she'd been resting. *How could you do this, Jane? How could you? What kind of beast have you become?* She struggled to breathe at the thought that she'd actually killed someone.

With a thumping heart, she went inside, washed her hands and took an apple from the fruit bowl as she tried to push the guilt away. *For Ryan. And for Emily. It had to be done.*

Forcing the thoughts from her mind, she let the instructions drift back in – it was nearly one whole month since she'd made the first payment. Plopping herself down into a comfortable lounge chair, she placed a fat cushion behind her back. Her joints had recently become more painful and she fought back the discomfort and concentrated on that phone conversation,, remembering every word.

'There's a park in the centre of town, with a tree that has a hollow in the trunk. You can't miss it. On the morning of the speedway, put the cash in an envelope with a photo of the target and where they can be located in that hollow. Two months later to the day, deposit the final payment in the same place. You got that?'

This was day fifty-nine.

'Ahhhh, showered already? Have you had a busy day or did you just feel like resting?'

Bill allowed the front door to close quietly behind him and switched on the light as he entered the room. 'It's getting dark early these days. Soon, it'll be cold but it's not too bad at the moment.' He looked at the chair opposite Jane and was about to sit in it but, at the last moment, headed to the kitchen. The familiar sounds of the fridge opening and cupboard doors closing indicated dinner would soon be cooking.

'Tomorrow I'm going to contact Colleen, the real estate agent,' he said. 'I think she's the best person to sell our house and help us look for a new place. Look out Port Burnie, here we come!'

The crashing of dishes continued, and Jane tried hard to ignore the clatter. She wished dinner would arrive soon just so the noise would stop. Recently she'd noticed the annoyance of noise, and this worried her. Perhaps it was a sign of deterioration. She wasn't sure, but she was pleased her work was almost accomplished. *Tomorrow is the big day. It's exactly two months after the first payment. I need to deposit the cash in the hollow.*

***

Jane opened her mouth to say something at breakfast but before she could speak, Bill rose from his chair and began stacking dishes. 'I'm going to start cleaning the shed before I see Colleen. Then I can come back and fill the trailer for the tip.'

'Good. I'll go down the street and buy some cream for our morning coffee,' Jane said, setting her plan into action. She headed to the bedroom to dress in warm clothes and complete her usual chores so she wouldn't attract attention. As she pulled on her jacket, she considered that, with Bill outside, she could smuggle the envelopes into her deep pockets. Her guilt now pushed well out of reach, she almost had a spring in her step as she left the house and walked into the garage. Once, she used to walk to the shop, but Bill was accustomed to seeing her drive everywhere now, and she acknowledged that using the car was the new norm. As she shut the car door and started the engine, she took a deep breath. There was Ned in his joggers exercising before work. He looked up and waved to Jane as she backed out onto the road. The last thing she wanted was to see a policeman – she felt the guilt rush back to her face – and, in a few nanoseconds, realised she was starting to panic. *He can't read minds. He doesn't know what you're doing. All you need to do is keep calm and drive to the park and drop in the money. He'll know I need to drive everywhere now and that walking's out of the question, even such a short distance.* Breathing easier, she turned the corner and smiled as, in the rear vision mirror, Ned headed out of his gate to commence his daily run.

Within seconds, the town park came into view. Thankfully, it looked deserted. Jane allowed the vehicle to slowly come to a halt close to the curb. She alighted from the car, left her handbag on the seat, and walked purposefully towards the tree in the park's centre. Glancing furtively around as she almost reached the centre point, she noticed Ned jog into the park from the west. Her back stiffened at the thought he might see her if she deposited the money, then he'd want to know what it was for, so she waited. Ned jogged on past, smiling and puffing as he went. She thought it odd that he would bother to do a daily exercise session when there were no other officers to record he was staying fit. *Dedication,* she put it down to, wishing she was able to jog.

When Ned had gone to the far edge of the park, and while his back was to her, she swiftly pulled the envelopes out of her pocket and dropped them in the gaping wooden hole. Then she turned and trundled away, looking back only once to make sure they had fallen deep enough not to be seen. Her mouth felt tight and dry; her head told her to hurry up and run, which made her chuckle silently – run? – she could barely walk – so she controlled the urge, and strolled purposefully back to the car. Soon she was motoring along the street towards home. Only then did she look around but nothing was out of the ordinary. She sighed as her house came into sight.

Oh, damn it! You've forgotten the bloody cream! Instantly, she turned around and headed for the local shop, trying to muster as much normality as she could, passing Ned again on his homeward leg.

A few minutes later, the coffee percolator bubbled and popped at the suburban house in Carinya, tension and fear mingling in the air with the steam from the coffee. Cold beads of sweat ran down Jane's arms and trembling legs. She toddled to the bathroom to compose herself before Bill walked in and saw her in this anxious state – he could read her behaviours like he read his newspaper each day.

***

A week later, Ned remembered seeing Jane drive down the street quite early in the morning, which he'd thought nothing of. He'd had a chat with Bill at the same time that day and had enquired after Jane's health, knowing it was compromised. In a small country town like Carinya, everyone knew everyone's business and sometimes others knew neighbours' secrets. Ned and his wife Lola made it a priority to stay as private as possible, the other townsfollk attributing this to being good citizens who maintained a strict sense of privacy and confidentiality. Maybe it was even important for his job.

It wasn't easy for Ned and Lola to fly under the radar in a parochial place like South Australia. But they tried, and mostly were successful, especially when it came to the details of Ned's transfer from Adelaide. And that was how it was going to stay.

'I'm just going out,' Lola said bluntly as she walked towards the car parked in the driveway.

On hearing her words, Ned turned suddenly and stopped putting away the garden tools. 'Why do you need to take the car? Why can't you walk? It's not far to the shops,' he said in the usual sharp tone he used when talking to her. 'We don't need to wear out the car!'

She glared at him, her lips tightening, not at all surprised at his brusque manner, though she had noted he spoke nicer to her when they had company. She'd excused his behaviour long ago, which others had told her was rude, bordering on abusive. She blamed this on his difficult job on the police force and his forced transfer from Adelaide Headquarters, even though others thought he was doing a brilliant job.

Indeed, Ned regularly congratulated himself on the excellent job he did, bringing home the 'extra dollars' that he then splurged on the races and other such pursuits. But others higher up in the police ranks who noticed used words like 'bribe' or 'misappropriation'. Ned and his colleagues had become angry when the bosses accused them of stealing as a servant, of white collar crime and then, horror of horrors, corruption! Most were offered transfers to undesirable locations and Ned's name had been on the top of the list for a move far, far away from the city. He'd thought of objecting, but knowing it could be proven he had sideline businesses and that he could fly under the radar better from afar, he'd willingly accepted a move to the country. Lola hadn't wanted to leave the city and had noticed since then he'd had unexplained bouts of anger and mood swings. Occasionally, he'd even raised his hand to her when she hadn't conformed to his ideas. Over the recent years, she'd learnt to become subservient, obeying him without question. And now, like a wounded sparrow, she shut the car door and moved inside to return to her chores, losing yet another day of interaction with other Carinya residents. She felt totally subdued.

That day, Bill had been within earshot and had heard the hostile tone Ned used when reprimanding Lola. He'd occasionally suspected Ned of being engaged in subversive actions and having different character traits, but their neighbourly chats had been friendly enough, albeit superficial. It was always a safe bet to talk about the weather and the football, Bill thought as he ambled away from the fence and moved towards his own safe space near his home. He'd turned the knob of the front door to find Jane standing with her jacket over her arm like she was ready for some action, or coming back from some. She placed the jacket, now devoid of its bounty, on the back of a chair, so peace reigned. The deed had been done and she could now relax.

'Have you been talking to Ned? Is he still as crazy as ever? Who would be a policeman today?' she muttered as she turned and went into the kitchen.

'Oh well, I know what you mean, but during our conversation, he made a weird suggestion. I didn't expect anything exceptional but when I told him I was going to the Real Estate agent, he became agitated and fidgety. I don't think he wants us to move, which I initially thought was quite endearing.'

'Really?' Jane replied. She leaned over to move the cups into position and looked at the clock, her mind racing as she wondered if the envelope had been removed from the tree in the park. 'So did he have anything enlightening to say or did he merely complain about something as usual?'

'Well, you're not going to believe this, but he actually wants to buy our house. I told him I was going to see Colleen to have a valuation done sometime soon, and he told me that he'll buy it when it's been valued, at whatever price is put on it.'

'Oh, my goodness! Is he serious? What's going on?'

'He said he's nearing retirement and feels sure his next service contract won't be renewed. He wants to stay in Carinya but he'll have to move out of the police accommodation if he retires. It sounds like he wants to retire before his contract expires. He's faced with two choices: he can either retire or not have his position renewed. It's the same result either way.'

'I see. Not happy prospects for Ned?'

Bill nodded. 'I told him I'd get back to him after the valuation. That gives us time to consider the whole business. We don't have to do anything quite yet. But it's interesting how events can turn out.'

With steam rising from the cups Jane put before them, Bill sat and looked at Jane. *Oh well, at least we don't have to decide quite yet.* Each one of them had totally different thoughts about the future and now Ned and Lola looked like they could be part of it.

Chapter 11

To Sell or Not to Sell

'Bill, don't trust him! That Ned Lawson is sleazy. I don't know why, but when I've seen him at the speedway, he's very friendly with all those bikie rev heads. And he's dressed in his cop's outfit and strutting around like he's playing a role in a play or cop drama!'

John sat in Bill's kitchen looking serious, the muscles in his neck taut, his mouth tight. 'It looks every bit like he's the crook, and the others are his sidekicks ready to do anything for him and *would* do anything if the opportunity arose. Those types love to make a buck, which makes the environments they attend not a place for the faint-hearted or honest folk. When I work there, I'm outa there before I get accosted.'

John drew breath and looked down at the table, acutely aware his comments were not what his friends wanted to hear. He remembered Fay's request to help Jane find someone to sell her some weed, which, though illegal, was not such a crime in his eyes given her situation. He'd found a contact and given the details to Fay, who'd passed it on to Jane. They were both mindful of keeping the secret from Bill … from anyone really given their line of work. The less anyone knew, the better. And the last thing John wanted was Ned sniffing around like a bloodhound. He knew as well as anyone that the annual July Speedway in Carinya was a cesspool for criminals, meetings, and illegal deals going down. And Ned hovered all around it.

With her white dress clinging to her now thin body, Jane felt a cold wind entering the previously comfortable room. Was it real or was it her imagination? She didn't know whether Death had begun its invasion or whether she was just feeling tired, which had become the new norm for her these days. She moved uncomfortably in her chair and opened her mouth to speak.

'Look, at the moment, I'm fine, but any day now, the cancer could metastasise, and soon afterwards, my lungs will collapse, and I'll be struggling to survive. That's the point when I move into the palliative care phase, and I would like to spend my time in my own home, or at Donna's place where the palliative care team can visit each day. A quick sale would be the way to go because Palliative Care teams don't come to Carinya very often.' Tears filled her eyes and threatened to spill over, but before they could, she hurried from the room.

'You can see why I'm keen for a quick sale, but slippery Ned could be a problem. I guess we just express our concerns to Colleen, so she ensures sale documents are legal and fully binding. So, he wants to live here in Carinya when he's finished with the Police Force ... you can't say it won't be an easy move shifting right next door. So what if he's friendly with the rev heads at the Speedway.' Bill heaved a deep sigh and concentrated on the table surface as John related numerous ways Bill could get cheated. And Ned's desire to buy the home was something he needed to be careful about.

'I heard he was a top cop in Adelaide ...' he went on. 'There has to be a reason he was transferred all the way out here ... to get him away from .... what?'

'Perhaps he's corrupt,' said Jane who had returned to the room. Bill marvelled at the position she'd taken in the face of her mortality as she marched stoically back in knowing she was on a path all creatures must travel. She astounded all those around her as she maintained the demeanour of total composure, with only the briefest of breakdowns, when tears sometimes flowed.

'Just quietly, I have no doubt, but no proof, he's corrupt. He *chooses* to move bush to serve in a small country town? I don't believe so. Nahhh, he was shifted by the big boys for some reason. Now, this is his turf and buying your house would ensure he retains his contacts. And when he's no longer a cop …! What's Carinya going to be like?'

The three friends sat in silence as the clock ticked loudly in the adjoining room. It was late in the afternoon before they could enter into another conversation. So much that needed to be said remained unsaid, but an air of intimate friendship had settled in the house, each wishing to suspend that moment in time.

***

Michael and Ryan travelled to their parents' house the following weekend, curious about how their father had cited 'something to discuss'. They were not surprised when the sale of the house was brought into the conversation as soon as Jane wasn't present.

'Look, Dad, what's it matter whether he's a crook or not? For you, the priority is Mum, and she's been having numerous ups and downs lately … her condition could deteriorate rapidly at any time … maybe soon. I'll bet, though, that old Ned will dictate his own terms and conditions knowing your reason for selling. You'll need to watch him, but you know that. Shall I gather some intel on him? I do have contacts.'

'Mike, leave that kinda stuff alone!' Ryan growled. He knew his brother had contacts; he obtained his weekly stash from someone, somewhere, but now wasn't the time to do anything underhanded. 'Dad, just do what you see fit,' he added. 'Yep, sell the house, and if Ned wants to buy it, put a high price on it.'

Bill looked from son to son, the lines on his face deepening as he leant forward in his chair. At Ryan's words, relief washed over him briefly as he acknowledged the enormity of the task ahead. Oh well, at least a decision had been made and now all he had to do was put his plan into action.

The following morning, the boys departed from Carinya and, as they travelled back to Port Burnie, each had different thoughts racing through their heads. Ryan appreciated the proximity of extended family for Emily and, being an only child, she was accustomed to seeking company in nearby houses. The quietness could be attributed to their mother's health, but Mike dwelt on Ned's reputation while Ryan considered his wife's behaviour. Jodie hadn't been seen or heard from for some time and he was starting to worry now that she hadn't been back to collect her things. And the truck driver was still in town and working, so where was Jodie? He still felt furious. She'd abandoned Emily – *how can a mother just up and leave her child like that? … like it doesn't matter!* And Jane and Bill were putting themselves out to come and care for Emily. His fury mounted the more he thought of her and her carefree lifestyle. Then he realised he hated her, and his fists had tightened at the thought. His brow deepened with every second he thought of her, and soon, he realised he'd need to control his thoughts and focus on the present, focus on the challenges of Emily and his work. He looked forward to his parents' arrival but knew it was only a temporary solution.

Soon he felt the speed decrease as Port Burnie came into view. The car purred along the street, and there, in the distance, was Mike's house with an unfamiliar car outside. He hoped it wasn't a druggie's car but then realised he was obsessing, given the conversation he'd had with his father about a possibly corrupt policeman.

'Who's that?' he murmured to Mike.

'Rest easy, bro. I don't know. But don't worry. No one knows where I live if you're thinking something sinister. A weekly drug deal isn't a big thing to worry about. Happens all the time. In fact, I need to go to the pub later today, so I can't dilly-dally around now.' He turned the engine off and stretched.

Michael pulled a key from his pocket as he opened the car door. 'Come on in, Ryan, and we'll structure a plan for work next week. We've got a good crew for a couple of days, which is good, but we need to look at the budget sometime soon and start preparing the end of the financial year reports. We're late again and Steven will be contacting us soon.'

The brothers knew Steven, their accountant, well. A friendly sort of guy, roughly the same age as Michael and Ryan, he gave the brothers good advice. The three of them had grown up together, and they all had a healthy attitude towards common sense and the law.

For the rest of the afternoon, the two poured over receipts and invoices like a bird making a nest, collecting the relevant parts and putting the rubbish to one side to discard. Soon all the pertinent papers were stapled together, and other documents were fastened by a bulldog clip. 'Tax work done,' Michael said. 'Grab a couple of stubbies out of the fridge, Ryan, before I go out. I think we've completed a good day's work and deserve it. Then you can pick up Emily before dark.'

With his hair streaking over his forehead, Michael leant back in the armchair and plonked his feet on the footstool. He flicked his hair back and gazed out the window. 'Poor Mum. And poor Dad too,' he muttered as Ryan flicked the top off the bottles. They both took a long slurp before speaking.

Ryan spoke first. 'So you reckon Ned's crooked?'

'I don't reckon, mate. I know it. I can sniff it out, but I wasn't telling the old man that. He's got enough to worry about. Old folks are vulnerable and it's our job to ensure they get the best treatment possible. Don't worry, I'll keep my eye on Ned. He's just a small-time cop in a small country town. But I reckon you need to keep your eye more on Jodie.' Michael didn't even draw breath. 'What a tramp she is. Where's she gone now?'

Ryan stiffened and started to think evasively. Then he changed his mind and looked steadily at his brother as his face flushed with colour. 'Who knows. Not me, but I can tell you, I'm as wild as hell. Look how she's deserted Emily! Luckily Emily has stopped asking after her. I'm pleased the folks are coming soon so we can assume the pretence of a normal home. But for how long? ... I don't know.' He cleared his throat and looked away in disdain, his jaw clenched. 'Anyhow, I'd better head for home,' he said, finishing his drink. 'Actually, I'd like to walk home but I'll have to be quick to pick up Emily and then do all the parent stuff. Some fresh air is what I feel like but hey, that's not a choice for me now.'

Soon the two men crunched across the gravel towards Michael's car. It was a new moon so blackness surrounded their steps as they moved in quick succession. How ironic, Ryan thought as he reflected on the darkness enveloping him. Somehow, the evening air encouraged the smell of gardens, and Ryan found it pleasant to sniff the eucalyptus, combined with the sea air. It felt reassuring in a strange kind of way. Somewhere in the distance, a truck could be heard carrying its heavy load, just like Ryan himself.

***

Emily entered the room as Ryan prepared an evening meal for two in the cosy kitchen. Somewhere in the distant background a noise sounded, and Ryan looked up from his domestic task. 'Was that a phone I heard ringing, Em?'

Emily turned to her father and looked at the soiled washing lying in disarray on the floor. 'It was a noise on the TV, Dad.' She gathered the clothes and took them into the laundry before setting the table. Ryan insisted on this duty as it embedded a sense of normality. With Jodie being away, it created the illusion she was momentarily absent.

Chapter 12

Jodie Formally Declared Missing

'I found Mum's phone!'

Emily, sensitive and intelligent, gauged the look on her father's face as he turned from the kitchen bench. He looked shocked, as she prayed he would be. 'It must have slipped down between the cushions on the lounge,' she said, trying to turn it on, but the battery was flat.

Time hung in the air as Ryan lurched towards a chair and plopped into it. At that hour of the morning, the hallway was illuminated from the bedroom light, the sun still struggling to take hold. A cold chill swept over Ryan when he heard Emily's words and he felt suddenly airless, nauseous. He needed to regain composure, for Emily's sake, as the appearance of Jodie's phone raised his concerns considerably.

'Mum must have left it behind. Or perhaps she left in a hurry.'

'She never leaves home without her phone! … 'Em, can you finish off here and get yourself ready for school? I'll drive you today and remember Gran and Grandad will be here later to pick you up from school.'

Emily did as requested as Ryan needed to call Mike and tell him to take the boat out today without him.

A cold wind settled around him as he and Emily walked to the car, last night's dew leaving moisture like a calling card warning of the approaching winter. It clung to the plants, and the damp, dilapidated outside table looked bleak and lonely. Ryan forced himself to concentrate on his driving and leave the Jodie business behind for the interim, but foremost on his mind was returning home and deciding what to do next.

His heart raced and his hand shook as images flew into his mind, images he didn't want to revisit.

***

On returning home, he searched for Jodie's car keys, found them in her top drawer, and unlocked her car. When he saw the familiar shoulder bag on the passenger's floor, he knew something was definitely wrong. She would never leave without her phone and here was her carry-all, something else she would never leave behind. He looked in the car boot and there was a shopping bag from Gloria's Boutique, inside it an expensive new shirt, waiting to be taken into the house and smuggled into the wardrobe after he'd gone to work. She did it so often.

His head shaking, he butt-leaned against the fender and swore, loudly, then rocked with pent-up rage, despair, and uncertainty.

When Jane and Bill arrived several hours later, Ryan was in the bedroom, frantically inspecting Jodie's clothes in the wardrobe. But nothing was missing, nothing at all.

'Slow down, son,' Bill said, grasping Ryan's arm. 'What is it? What's wrong?'

Words spilled out of Ryan's mouth like an unleashed geyser. 'Her phone … this morning we found her phone! She never leaves home without it. And there's other stuff … I don't think she ran off, Dad. I … I think something's happened!

'Here, sit down … calm down. Let's go through this.' Bill sat him down and repeated what Ryan had said, checking and gauging his own understanding. Finally, as Jane stood mute and watched, feeling a cold chill wash over her, Bill suggested they phone the police.

***

Finishing his phone call with Ryan, Michael swore silently. *Of course, Ryan thinks it's an emergency — everything's an emergency in his frail little head. Damn it, now I'll be short-staffed on the boat, so all the crew will have to work harder, and that'll make them grizzle.* He grabbed his car keys from the old table and let the door bang loudly as he left.

As he drove towards the wharf, he noticed his crew hanging around waiting for him. Ryan's phone call had delayed him and now he'd need to be in apology mode before the boat even started. He tried to dismiss thoughts of Ryan as he stepped up onto the boat. Others followed, and soon the engine started and they were on their way to the open sea, ready for a morning's fishing. Pots were baited and ropes coiled to facilitate dropping them off in the designated places. The GPS coordinates were set as the distance from shore increased and they sped off before the breeze came in to disrupt the ease of the operation. They were dropping some pots and pulling others, this the routine Michael had developed for the most successful catch. Keeping the crew contented was a major part of Michael's job now, and he felt even more hostile towards Ryan as the engine roared and the boat bounced across the rising swell.

Quite clearly, Ryan's dilemma had made Michael's job harder, and he wasn't quite sure how long he could make allowances for a partner who wasn't pulling his weight. He'd take a serious look at the situation after Steven completed the tax return for the financial year.

Several hours later, as Michael allowed the boat to almost drift towards the marina, he could see Garry loading gear onto a jetty, and decided to chat before returning home to ascertain what kind of emergency Ryan had referred to. The fenders slowly scraped the jetty as the crew, ropes at the ready, prepared to tie off. Still at the wheel, Michael looked over to see Garry waving in the distance. The breeze had swung around so the boat required considerable strength from the crew to tie it firmly into its pen so the catch could be wheeled ashore to load into containers.

There was his truck and driver, waiting as instructed, for its load. The routine worked efficiently and Michael shut his eyes briefly to relieve their tiredness. He rubbed his salt-streaked face, marking the end of a working day, knowing it would happen all over again tomorrow. Finally, he stepped up over the gunnel and onto the wooden jetty.

Garry still worked some distance away, so Michael strode towards him, happy to stretch his legs and feel the wind on his face. He yawned and stretched his arms as he walked, realising the hours on the boat had made his back ache. He'd need a heat pack on it when he went home.

'What's up, young Mike?'

'I think we made it back just before the breeze whipped up. Always good to see that truck load up and take those crays away … really satisfies my bank account.'

Michael studied Garry's movements and realised how age catches up with everyone. His uncle moved slower these days and he noted the considerable effort it took to lift and carry things. Sweat had beaded on his forehead and he huffed to catch his breath. Michael expected the grizzling to start but, to his surprise, Garry stopped working and wiped his brow.

'Think I'll call it a day. Actually, I've had a pretty good run this week. Two docks installed, as the pile driver did all the drilling without a hitch. Makes a change!'

Garry took out his water bottle and swallowed furiously, his strong fingers strangling the soft plastic container. 'Why don't you come around home for a drink? I reckon we could both do with one. I put some beers in the fridge last night. Donna's got a meeting until late so we could even warm up a pizza. What do you say?'

'Brilliant idea. I just need to log these blokes' hours at the office and then I'm ready to go.'

Leaving the marina, Michael strode towards the office when suddenly a four-wheel drive whizzed passed him, just a little too closely.

'What the hell!' he called out, but the driver kept accelerating along the bitumen and seconds later created a deliberate backfire. Michael didn't see who it was so, when he arrived at the office, he told the staff what had happened. 'The guy was well over the limit for the marina … he's a menace to society!'

'Would you like to see the CCTV footage so you can identify the offender?' the office girl asked

So Michael watched the replay of the last ten minutes, marvelling at the technology. While some of the footage looked blurry, the camera had taken clearer footage of the driver's face.

Michael swore. 'Angry Andy! He's one of the truck drivers. Can you rewind it? I need to be sure.' So he reviewed the footage, slowly, so he could be certain. And there it was again. Even though it was at an angle, there was no doubt this was the same driver who'd given Jodie a lift some time ago.

Michael wondered if the near-miss had been intentional and couldn't shake the animosity as the face of angry Andy stared at him. *Of course, it was intentional!* Michael felt like reporting the incident to Police. *What a wally! But why does Andy have an issue with me?*

By the time Michael arrived at Garry's place, the light was fading. He relayed the incident to his uncle as they sat in comfy chairs sipping cold beer. 'Some of these truck drivers have a grudge against things. Don't take it personally. Perhaps he knows you're related to Jodie and Jodie dumped him. It may be connected, but I always say these kinds of blokes just lost at cards. Perhaps it was just random? Don't think about it again. Lots of deadbeats around as we both know.'

They let it go and instead discussed the cricket. As the dark of a winter evening set in, Michael decided to visit Ryan and see what the big emergency was all about. When Garry offered him some pizza to take home, he accepted.He'd decided *Ryan and Emily might be hungry, and the gesture might appease his touchy brother. Ryan is just so needy.*

He slammed the car door after twisting his body into the cab and cursed. He'd left the window down all day so now it was cold, and the breeze whipped around his ears before he could wind it up. Before long, he turned into Ryan's street and there his mouth dropped open. His heart started racing. In front of him were vehicles. *What's a police car doing at Ryan's? Is it for Ryan, or is it for one of his neighbours?* He put his foot down harder on the accelerator, his mind suddenly alert. *What's happening?* As he left his vehicle and hurried up the driveway, two uniformed police officers walked towards him, heading for their car.

'What's happening?'

'I suggest you ask folks inside,' one replied, and they kept crunching the gravel loudly as they strode in the half-light towards the front gate. *It's like they don't care*, Michael thought, *or maybe it's nothing to worry about. Or nothing they need to worry about.* He didn't know the nature of their visit to Ryan, but he was sensible enough to realise they distanced themselves from incidents to be able to do their job. But Michael *did* worry! This was his family inside! His mind went into overdrive, and he hurried towards the back door, almost shouting at Ryan, who stood on the verandah, watching the police leave.

'What's happening, bro?'

Then he caught himself, recomposed with relief that he could talk to his brother before seeing his parents and his niece inside. 'Is it Mum? Have you called an ambulance?'

'No, it's not Mum. It's Jodie. She's missing,' Ryan answered, his voice trembling. Fear was in his eyes when he looked at Michael.

Even in the dim light of the verandah, Michael could see the tightness on Ryan's face, but couldn't help himself. 'Of course, she's missing! She's a tart! She's always missing, bro … always causing chaos around here, so what's new?' Then Michael remembered his sick mother inside, and lowered his voice. It was impossible to hide that he hated Jodie now, especially for causing mayhem when his mother was so ill.

'No, Mike. She's officially been declared missing now … by the cops.'

'We don't need to upset Mum with this.'

'Mike, it's more serious.' Ryan's voice rose. 'I think they suspect foul play. Her bag and phone are here. Her wardrobe is undisturbed. And her bank account is untouched.'

Michael's eyes narrowed as he took it all in, but he couldn't believe what he was hearing. While it gave him ironic pleasure to learn Jodie was missing, this knowledge was not what he wanted to hear. In the twilight, raindrops falling softly on the roof fractured the silence. The two men stood, Michael's eyes wandering over the dilapidated garden, which he felt was Jodie's responsibility – she was good for nothing. But from

Ryan's statements sprang questions, serious questions that raised issues of criminality. Michael stared ahead and, as the smells of neighbours' cooking invaded his nostrils, he was amazed how normality reigned elsewhere when Ryan's world had just collapsed.

Reluctantly, Michael spoke. 'Has there been an accident?'

Time dragged on, and a kind of wildness enveloped Michael's mind, all types of possibilities flashing through his thoughts. Then he realised Ryan was saying something, and listened.

'I don't know,' Ryan muttered, shaking his head.

As the enormity of the situation intensified, they braced themselves, opened the back door and Michael steeled himself, ready to greet his parents, and Emily, as best he could.

Chapter 13

Ned Buys a House

When Jane and Bill Thompson's car slowly left the driveway in Carinya at noon, Ned suspected they were heading to Port Burnie. He watched them depart and decided he'd share the news of the house sale with Lola when she made lunch for him. After all, she would need to sign documents and he felt unusually cheerful. With the Thompsons away, they could sneak around and have a better look at the place through windows and investigate more deeply their soon-to-be property. The quick walk-through he'd had with the agent hadn't given him enough time to really check out the place in detail.

He had no doubt Bill and Jane would accept his offer. Who else would want to come and live in a tiny rural place in South Australia that had zero lifestyle or career potential? He hadn't wanted to live here either but powerful people had coerced him, and now it was time for payback.

Ned leant back in his comfy chair and put his feet on the footstool as he swallowed his last morsel of sandwich. Lola vacuumed around him, the constant buzzing noise reminding him of a time in the city when policing consisted of liaising with gangs on the street and coming to agreements. He'd spent a lot of time cultivating friendships, later claiming this led to drug busts, but the reality was, when the police raided particular houses to make arrests, the inhabitants were either absent or pleaded ignorance. Somehow, individuals knew there was going to be a raid. It was some time before Ned's name was put forward to the Corruption Squad, and he'd been given choices. One of those was a stint at Carinya. It didn't matter what reasons Ned put forward, and he had plenty, the Commission ignored his case. Lola knew none of this as Ned had decided that, like lots of things in life, the less individuals who knew, the better.

The bonus of Carinya was the annual speedway event, which attracted the criminal element from all around Australia, including some of his past associates from Melbourne. Initially, he couldn't believe his good luck and hiding behind the police uniform provided an extra layer of status and secrecy.

A decade of good fortune from these associations allowed him to save a lot of money. He'd contemplated resigning, but he needed to live close by to the new copper to cultivate the perception of friendship. And how better to do that than from the Thompson's house next door to the new cop's house, one house away from the Police Station? Perfect situation!

'Can you please move your stool, Ned?'

He had almost dozed off when these words filtered into his consciousness and disturbed his pleasant thoughts. He gruffly accepted what he had to do and then decided it was time to discuss the upcoming purchase with his wife. He blurted it straight out.

'We're going to buy the Thompson place next door. You'll need to be there to sign the papers when the time comes.'

Her mouth fell open, but she caught herself and simply nodded.

'Let's go and have a look through the windows so you can see what we're buying.' Soon, he was opening the front gate and striding down the rickety path towards the backyard, Lola following meekly after, yet she took a fair interest in looking in windows as they went. Ned led the way and occasionally found a window without the blinds drawn and stealthily peered into the privacy of the Thompson's home without any shame. Putting his finger to his lips, he continued around to the backyard and looked into the shed, trying to see as much as he could through its dark spaces. Then he tried the latch and almost laughed to find the door unlocked, so he stepped inside confidently, trying not to touch anything that would mark his presence. He left all tools and goods in situ to show no disturbance. *Good old, Bill,* he thought. *Perhaps he may leave some equipment behind. And with a sick wife, he'll probably want a quick sale, to my benefit.*

'Let's go home. We've seen enough,' he said suddenly, holding his hand and smiling into Lola's eyes. 'But let's just have a look to see where we'll put our fridge. I think you can see through the curtain … unless we can find an outside key.'

Much to their surprise, they found a key, very predictably hidden under the back door mat. Ned used his handkerchief to hold it as he unlocked the back door and, when Lola looked at him and frowned, he responded with, 'No fingerprints.'

Lola smiled and gullibly accepted his words, yet she felt guilty, but knew not to mention this to Ned. It would make no difference, and she knew he liked to impress her, or anyone else who needed to be impressed by the many tricks of the trade he'd learnt from years on the beat. So, slipping off their shoes, they snuck inside the house and went from room to room.

In Jane's bedroom, they found medical paraphernalia, which they stared at intently. 'Clearly she's got all her gear with her, but I wonder how much longer she's got?' Ned said, putting his glasses on so he could read the label. 'It doesn't matter. It's all details we don't need to know. Let's get outa here.'

Ned guided Lola out of the bedroom and along the passage. 'Just for the hell of it, I'm going to see what they've got in their fridge,' Ned said as he levered open the fridge with a tea towel, still intent to not leave any traces of them in the house.

Then they left, a dog suddenly barking in the distance as Ned and Lola closed the front gate. They'd seen enough of their future purchase and the conversation reverted to Jane's health.

It wasn't long before Ned and Lola Lawson began speculating on how long they'd need to wait before Ned retired from the Force. They would then need to create a plan for moving and establishing a new chapter in their lives. The planning was all in Ned's head; Lola continued with cleaning and cooking, with remarkedly little thought for Jane's predicament or the house next door.

***

In Port Burnie, Jane's outlook had progressed surprisingly well, given she'd just heard the news about Jodie's disappearance. Of course, she felt devastated for poor Emily, but seeing her plan unfold gave her an absolute sense of relief. *It's happening!* And she half-smiled, unaware Bill was watching her. Her smile made him frown.

With Ryan outside on the verandah updating Michael with the news, and Emily having a shower, Jane and Bill had a moment to share in private.

'The police interview must have been gruelling. Poor Ryan looks distraught,' Bill said as he carried their overnight bag into the guest room. 'I think Ryan's yet to consider he may be the prime suspect.'

Jane squeezed her eyes shut as she sat on the bed. She felt exhausted and her back pain had been increasing in recent days, but she wasn't going to divulge that to Bill. Now her relief about Jodie's disappearance was etched with concern about Ryan's interview with the police. 'Why would the Police accuse or suspect Ryan?' She shook her head. Not once had she thought about the implications of Jodie going missing. Her breath caught in her throat, and she closed her eyes and tried to close her mind to what could happen to Ryan.

As Bill unpacked their case, Jane listened to the silence in the room and smelt the odour of old wood furniture. It reminded her of her grandparent's home when she visited so many years ago. *How ironic,* she thought, *that I can smell it now in my son's house. Is it an omen that some things never go away?* Then she indulged her fantasy to pleasantly remind herself that her $20,000 was paid out to ensure Ryan's problem *would* go away! This was her dream come true and now she needed to remain coy to avoid any suspicious notions Bill may have. His voice was husky and tired as he answered her question.

'The husband is always the first line of inquiry. He's generally the first suspect. I'm not sure if they asked him for details about his relationship with Jodie. They would have to consider Jodie's absences peculiar, wouldn't you say?' Bill closed the overnight case and looked away, sat on the opposite side of the bed and his hands tightened around his kneecaps as he bent down to remove his shoes. 'It doesn't really sound like a loving marriage.'

A mixture of emotions swam around in Jane's mind, and she closed her eyes. The last thing she wanted was suspicion to fall on Ryan.

***

Ryan leaned on the patio table as he spoke with Michael. 'I can't believe they think I'm a person of interest. How does that happen? I gave the cops her mother's phone number and suggested they call her but they didn't seem interested.' He turned and looked for the remote for the verandah heater.

'She's been missing five weeks, bro. Did you tell the police she often goes bush? Not quite sure if it helps or not!' Michael smiled grimly.

'Course I did. But by the look on their faces, I don't think they believed me.'

'Well, the delay in letting them know probably hasn't helped you. And they'll now go through the motions and tick the boxes. Don't worry, bro. She'll probably turn up one day soon without considering the trouble she's caused everyone. Isn't that the usual pattern?'

Bill joined them, looking showered and fresh. 'I've put a casserole in the oven to warm so we can at least eat. I doubt anyone will be hungry but we need to keep up appearances for Emily's sake. Your mother's laying down resting. She has her eyes shut but I'm sure she'll find sleeping difficult tonight. We all will.'

'Look, guys,' said Michael, who in emergencies assumed the role of family leader, 'we'll need to make a plan. Ryan, I think you need to keep working with me on the boat and Dad can look after Emily and Mum. Keep busy, mate, and avoid thinking about Jodie. I need you on the boat and we can think of a long-term plan later. Dad can manage here, can't you, Dad.' It was more of a statement than a question and Bill nodded to accommodate Michael's suggestion.

Soon, dinner smells wafted to them and, as it was served, a feeling of normality pervaded the house.

'Mum's asleep still so I won't disturb her,' Bill told them, quietly concerned about Jane's deterioration – her loss of appetite seemed to feature regularly. She was lethargic and constantly tired. They had learnt to be together without speaking, and Bill could detect Jane's downfall quite easily. Excusing himself from the table, he went to check on her. He was quietly pleased Michael had taken charge and that Ryan could lean on his brother for support. It was good, too, that Mike evoked in Ryan a sense of significance and purpose but for the Police to consider Ryan a person of interest was disturbing. He was too emotionally involved to realise the Police were merely doing their jobs and the situation drained him.

Bill fell asleep readily that night and slept fitfully until woken by a phone ringing. By the time he found his phone, it had stopped ringing and Bill soon saw it was Ned who'd rung. His heart raced as he imagined all sorts of emergencies so he dialled back immediately.

'Ned, mate, what's up? Just wait a minute.'

Not in the mood to discuss pleasantries, he made his way outside to avoid waking Jane who, surprisingly, slept soundly. The twinge of panic was clear in his voice and he closed the back door softly as he focused on what Ned had to say.

'Take it easy; take it easy, Bill. I've been talking to Colleen about the sale of your house. Lola and I have agreed to pay the price you're asking. It's a fair price and, at this stage, I'm not sure when I'd have the finance available, but I'll make the offer unconditional, so you know it's genuine.' Ned's conversation halted as he drew breath. 'How's that for some good news for you? Colleen will give you all the info.'

Bill, frowning slightly at Ned's admission, thanked him for his phone call and agreed to call the real estate office that morning to confirm the details and what it meant. As his mind engaged with the subject, he felt his stomach lurch. A grim smile tightened his lips, yet he tried to push back his emotions. It was only a house, after all. But he knew it was more. Was he signing off on Jane's life and preparing for the future? Such thoughts of guilt raced through his head in the early fresh morning. He tried to remain positive and, after a few minutes, entered Ryan's house ready to share the news. It was what they wanted, after all, wasn't it?

He felt numb from Ned's phone call for some time and remained sitting in his chair staring at the floor until Emily reminded him it was time for school.

Chapter 14

Donna Assumes Her Role

Donna drove home with many thoughts in her mind after a long day supervising the wards where she worked as an anaesthetist nurse. Surgeries were cancelled due to staff absences, and patients had understandably been upset. Donna lamented the days when staff were happy to work overtime simply for more money. Now nurses wanted a balanced lifestyle where home, work and play were all considered equally important, and Donna reluctantly supposed they were.

Now, as she approached retirement, she felt tired. The repetitive nature of her work made her look at her watch, quite often late in the afternoon, when she would count the hours before she could leave to go home.

Suddenly, the Bluetooth in her car registered that her phone was ringing, and she jerked her thoughts back to concentrate on the call. It was Michael, and she pressed the appropriate button to connect.

'Look, Donna, I'm coming around to your place on my way home as I want to catch up with you, and Garry when he gets home. It's not quite an emergency but … …'

'I'll give him a call if you like, Mike. I'm in the car, as you can tell, and he's probably on his way home too.'

Michael was such a caring person so Donna assumed the news would be about Jane. She and Garry often commented on the way he assumed leadership during a crisis and took on the leadership during dilemmas, making sure they were handled with as much diplomacy as possible. With their own children, Lexie and Talia working overseas, it seemed like their nephews were their own sons. Of course, living close by ensured close connections, and she hoped her sister and Bill would sell their country home soon and come to live close by too.

Soon, her house came into view and she glanced left and right at the intersection as she wondered about Michael's phone call. Surely, he would have told her if Jane's condition had deteriorated. She glanced at the fuel gauge before turning off the engine, opened the driver's door and climbed out. She waited a moment, and soon Michael's car turned the corner into her street, followed by Garry's so Donna picked up her handbag and made her way to the front door, hoping the air inside wasn't freezing.

'You're not going to believe this, but Jodie's been officially declared missing,' Michael came straight out with it. Garry plopped down on a lounge chair; Donna drew in a breath and blew it out again. She turned to Michael, who shrugged. 'I shouldn't be so abrupt but there's no other way to say it.' He paused as the silence grew. 'When I checked up on Ryan yesterday, the Police had been there. Poor old Ryan was in a bit of a state.'

Michael paused. 'Mum and Dad stayed last night, too, to look after Emily. I believe they're going to be there for a while but who knows what's going to happen now.'

'Unbelievable, yet not unbelievable,' Donna said. The hum of the electric heater sounded as strain and tension hung in the air. Outside, a car roared past, the sound drifting off into the dusk. With an effort, Donna pushed herself up off the chair and moved to the fridge. 'Mike, we're having a curry. Would you like to stay? You must be hungry after a day's work too. We're all hungry and luckily, it's already made.'

Garry then stood and began to set the table while Donna warmed the dinner in a saucepan on the stove. 'Mike, what happens now? What did the Police say?'

'Well, they have listed her as missing just on the fact that her phone and handbag were still at home. Her clothes were undisturbed, and her bank accounts haven't been touched for weeks. Ryan suggested they ring Jodie's parents to see if she was there, but we're not sure what they will do. He wouldn't ring them before because Jodie's been spreading rumours that he'd been abusive to her and he didn't want a confrontation. He became instantly concerned when Emily found Jodie's phone. The battery was flat but, after charging it, no unusual calls were on it. No messages. I think it was at that point he rang the Police.'

They ate dinner almost in silence with the television sounding away softly in the background to normalise the situation. They watched the News on TV in case a bulletin came out about Jodie and were less interested in dinner, but each consumed the curry nevertheless and waited for time to pass. Subsequent talk was indirect and inconsequential, interrupted by pauses and long silences with no one really knowing what else to say. Jodie was missing – it was a simple as that.

To change the subject, Donna asked about Jane.

'Look, I think she's all right at the moment. I didn't see her last night as she was resting. Not sure if she ate dinner or not as she was on the bed after the trip from Carinya. Dad says she gets really tired now.'

Garry, washing the dishes, stopped to listen. Even to his untrained ear, he could sense Jane's progression towards the final stages but they would discuss this and palliative care after Michael went home. Donna continued folding the washing and thought about Mike's response.

That night, lying in bed, Garry began gently snoring but Donna kept thinking about Jane. All the signs were not good – loss of appetite, loss of weight and tiredness. At this stage, Jane's pain management strategy looked to be working, and Donna felt relieved, though her nursing experience told her it would be short-lived. For now, though, each day without pain was a bonus. She reflected on her knowledge of cancer and knew there were so many types of cell multiplication where something could change, so many variations as lives changed and it was not surprising oncologists were reluctant to provide details. Individuals would cling to information like fleas to a dog, and become angry when prognoses were wrong. Hence, the medical fraternity closed ranks and said very little to avoid patient disappointment. In hospitals, staff had been advised to minimise information to patients and refer them instead to their own doctors. In other words, let the doctors dictate and play God, not nurses. It was safer that way.

***

Donna opened her eyes in the dark and thought about a plan for Jane. 'Garry, I think we need to set up Lexie's room for Jane. It's not good for her to be at Ryan's place, dying, with Emily watching.'

Garry rolled over as he heard her voice. He had his hands loosely on the bedclothes and moved towards his wife in a bid to wake up. 'Good idea. Let's talk about it in the morning.' He promptly fell asleep and began snoring again.

So, it came to pass that Donna organised palliative care as a plan, and, although Jane wasn't yet at that stage, she knew it must be close, and prepared herself. She arranged a meeting with Jane and her doctor, and Donna had a further conversation with the hospital.

'We won't wait for life to become difficult, Jane. Bill can move your things into Lexie's room and he can sleep in Talia's room, next to yours. You'll have your own bathroom and we'll sleep upstairs.' Donna was dispassionate and reasonable, with all the traits of someone who was used to being in charge. Naturally, her medical background was a bonus and she was aware of Jane's mind weakening as her body wasted, but even she was unprepared for the suddenness.

It all happened one night when Jane's pain became unbearable and an ambulance was called. Sweat broke out on Jane's forehead and her speech became slurred and frantic.

***

When Jane returned to Donna's a few days later, ambulance officers wheeled her inside on a stretcher and assisted medical staff in lifting her onto her bed. An oxygen bottle was set up beside the bed, and a nasal cannula was fitted to help Jane breathe easier. Even though barely conscious, Jane heard voices. She felt like a wounded animal but was alert enough to remember the fate of Jodie. She was still missing and, at this stage, there was no news of her whereabouts.

Jane smiled inwardly, experiencing overwhelming relief. She was glad she had lasted long enough to know her plan had worked and, in her mind, she felt young and energised because of it. A new tranquillity entered the room in that no one knew of her plan and all the details involved. She took her sedatives and drifted off into a relaxed consciousness where she felt little else. When she conversed with Bill, she felt almost giddy with excitement and the family attributed her happiness to the drugs. Her mind, however, remained quite lucid for long periods and she enjoyed reminiscing with family members who, on and off, came to see her.

Week by week, her strength remained fairly constant despite the cancer racing through her body, and doctors were surprised. They warned Bill her state of euphoria would not last, and the end would come soon. Jane's face had softened with time and she knew she had to keep her strength up by eating, even when she didn't feel like it. Her skin became stretched out around her eyes and mouth as her blue eyes sank deeper into her face. She remembered the children as babies; she remembered their courtships and how much they laughed when they were young. School anecdotes she could recall with clarity as she relayed them to a tired Bill. As her eyes wanted to close, she fought to keep them open though she struggled to move her body in the bed. Her spirit was separating from her physical being and she needed to talk to participate in the world around her. Often, she would sleep instantly, exhausted, and only then could Bill awkwardly rise from the chair and attend to his own needs.

In the dim, familiar passage between the two bedrooms, Bill moved with the tiredness of an old man. *My God*, he thought, *how much longer can this keep on,* then he felt guilty and a lump formed in his throat. His wife was dying and all he could think of was his own exhaustion!

'Dad, you look absolutely buggered,' Michael blurted out as he let the back door slam. The cat made a quick dash out and narrowly avoided its tail being jammed in the door – it'd had a lot of practice running in and out of the kitchen. Bill looked up and nodded at Michael as he opened the fridge. He could hardly speak but his look of benevolence negated the need for words between them. A contented silence filled the room.

'I wonder, Dad, if you should do all the paperwork for the house sale with Colleen while Mum's still coherent. She's not going to last long like this; she'll go downhill pretty quick – that's assuming you're still happy with Ned buying the house.

Once Mum's gone, the whole process can get quite complex, I was told.'

Bill stared at the floor and focused on a worn patch near the doorway. That's how he felt, he realised; worn out. He looked up at Michael with watery eyes and realised he needed to become proactive in this situation. He took a deep breath and listened to the laboured breathing in the next room. Michael was right and Bill recognised the sense his son was making. Soon, this deep breathing would turn into a death rattle as the fluid etched its way further into Jane's lungs.

'You're right, Mike. I'll get my act together and go today.' *Somewhere along the line, I need to start thinking, and this is going to begin today,* he thought. He stretched his legs and looked out the window at the morning sky as he walked past the table and into the passage. In his room, he prepared for the trip to Carinya.

'Good on you, Dad. I'll have tea cooked for you at my place tonight. Just you and me. I'd better keep moving and so had you.'

Chapter 15

Documents Signed

Ned sat in the patrol car a few kilometres out of Carinya, listening to the radio and working on the daily crossword in the newspaper. He felt safe and contented sitting in his car. The sun was high and regularly peeped out to challenge the easterly wind. But Ned's car protected him from many elements, not only the weather.

He'd parked the car so it was quite visible to on-coming traffic thus enabling drivers to slow down to avoid a speeding fine. He smirked, knowing locals thought him a considerate, thoughtful cop but the truth was he just couldn't be bothered chasing down errant drivers to book them for speeding. He considered it his prevention programme, which also allowed him privacy to check emails, messages and take and make phone calls on his burner phone while his police phone remained on silent. He could while away a few hours doing this – he called it 'tending to business'.

Even Lola didn't know about his sideline ventures, and that was how he wanted it. He didn't even need to recruit nowadays as the winter Speedway event enabled him to work with blokes who wanted big money, and he knew how to make it and avoid detection and, therefore, jail time. He reflected for a few moments on how easy it was to make a living as a country cop, provided there were no impromptu dramas.

But soon, he wouldn't have the protection of the uniform and the patrol car, so he needed to get his affairs in order to enable his 'business' to continue as usual. And blow the big brass in Adelaide who couldn't prove a thing, yet transferred him to the outback … he was going to continue his payback. He knew police procedures, and over the years in Caryina he'd had a lot of opportunity to cultivate his quiet little business on the side without revealing his cover; he'd endeared himself to the community, which was an enormous benefit. For now, he'd record the number plates of passing vehicles so he could write information in his police diary. He also wanted to finish his crossword while he was out on the road.

Taking a deep breath, he opened his thermos and poured his morning coffee and was only halfway through drinking it when a Toyota Landcruiser approached in the distance, so he gulped it down and prepared to look like a cop at work.

'Well, well, well, it's my neighbour Bill.' Ned leant against the patrol car and took his sunglasses off as he looked at Bill across the car bonnet, a smile creeping across his haggard face. 'Good to see you, mate.'

By this stage, Bill had climbed from his car and stood next to it stretching his legs. The drive from Port Burnie was long and tiring and his back now ached, and his eyes were sore. He mumbled something about not wasting any more time and ran his hand through his hair, or what was left of it, and added, 'Looks like the rain's gone, though it has left a good amount of puddles.' He looked at the spoon drain on the side of the road and then back at Ned. Somehow, there was that self-assuredness Bill couldn't quite decipher in the man, but he attributed it to his own tiredness. This whole business with hospitals and Jane's illness was exhausting him, so Bill dismissed Ned and opened his car door. He wound down his window and prepared to drive away. 'Come over when you finish here and we can talk about the house sale.'

Bill felt relieved those words were now out and that relief flooded Ned's face.

'Sure thing, Bill.'

***

Later, as Ned knocked on Bill's back door, Bill looked up from making a sandwich for himself and invited Ned inside. 'Have a look through the house if you like so you can refresh your mind to what you're buying.'

Bill's comment caught Ned by surprise and he looked towards the passage as quickly as he could to hide his embarrassment. Bill continued making his sandwich as Ned played the innocent and polite home viewer. The kitchen was clean and Bill wiped down the bench and ate his sandwich while waiting for Ned to return.

'Do you think Lola will like the layout of the house?'

'Bill, she'll love having a home of our own rather than a government police house. It's all good, mate. Let's sign up the papers down at Colleen's. If you can accept that I pay you half now and then after Christmas, when I've resigned, I'll pay the balance. We can share the place until then, and you only surrender the title deeds after I pay the balance.'

Bill shrugged, then grinned and finished his sandwich. 'Sounds like a good plan, Ned. Let's go. And I get free Security while I'm away at Port Burnie.'

Later that day, Bill strolled around his home touching his favourite things, and feeling very aware that time was marching on. *I guess it's life*, he lamented silently. The irony was it had been Jane's lack of life that had driven the decision to sell and move to the coast.

At Colleen's, they had agreed on a long settlement to enable Ned to resign from the Police Force and arrange finance with his bank. As Ned suggested, Bill would retain the Certificate of Title until then and have access to his property. Bill now realised this was a most satisfactory arrangement for dealing with his belongings – he had nowhere to put them yet so leaving them in place was most logical. Though he did start to box up items to make room for Ned's, lingering on family photographs scattered throughout the rooms and gazing at images of a much younger Jane, he felt dreadful. Slowly, he prepared to end his reminiscing and sat down to watch television with a cup of tea.

Just as he started dozing off through the drone of the television, a banging came at the back door. *What does Ned want now?* he griped, waking with a start. Even though he'd signed the papers, something didn't quite sit easily with the shared arrangement yet and he didn't want to talk to Ned again today. *It's been enough for one day*, he reasoned. The banging sounded again and this time Bill jumped out of his chair as he recognised John's voice.

'Oh, thank God, it's you! Come on in,' and he opened the door widely.

John strolled in with drinks and take-away food, which he put on the table and sat down with Bill. A long night began with good friends sharing drinks and dinner.

'So, nosey Ned signed the Offer and Acceptance?'

Bill kept eating and couldn't look at John. 'Had to be done, mate. It's always difficult selling your home … but for Jane, we need to be in a decent-sized town. No palliative care down here.'

The moments passed with both men enjoying their food, as well as each other's company.

'When are you and Fay going to join us in the big city? Not that we'd describe Port Burnie as a big city. Guess it's just a big town. You could get work in Burnie. Just what is it you do for your job, John? Some kind of office work?' Bill had never received an answer to this question from John, despite it being asked often enough! He knew he did something with trucks and was always travelling back and forth in his car.

'Guess you've got a few bits and pieces to clear up in the house?' John dodged the question as if he hadn't been listening. 'Do you need a hand?'

'But, John, what is it all about?'

John wouldn't be drawn into specifics. He'd always passed it off laconically as 'clearing up a few bits and pieces for the government', at which time friends complained to him about the condition of the roads or lack of government services, but John remained largely evasive. Unlike others in the town, he didn't wear a uniform to identify himself, and gradually, folk had grown tired of delving. Eventually, John blended into the community, identifying as an innocuous government worker who, by and large, kept to himself.

***

If Ned had been peeping through the window, he would have seen two old friends in despair, eating and drinking, finally turning the television on to watch a football game. *So, Bill is staying overnight,* Ned realised. He didn't need to peep through a window to fathom that, and the familiar car in the driveway belonged to John, a friend of Bill's. A quiver ran across his skin as he realised he didn't quite trust John. *Still,* he reasoned, *it isn't John who's selling the house. But I like Bill – he's dithery and naive.* And because he didn't trust John, he watched from a distance. *As for the women, they don't figure in the equation.* Indeed, as a wife, Lola suited him just fine. She knew when to keep quiet and out of the way.

'Lola, bring me another beer.' And like that, Ned continued to watch the football on television, too, with his feet up on the footstool and the old rug covering his jeans to keep warm. Soon, he'd allow Lola to turn on the heating but it was only early winter, so he reasoned the cold weather was yet to arrive and etch its way into Carinya.

By morning, a storm had cleared, and Bill began his drive away from his home, which was no longer really his home now. He tried hard to deal with his morbid thoughts, but his head ached, his mouth was dry and he knew he'd had too much to drink the night before. He even struggled to remember their conversations. John was keen to reminisce whereas Bill had been engaged in the football match. Winning games was important and it provided Bill with the welcome distraction he would need in the months ahead. He had a massive task ahead as he moved forward, and approaching the depths of winter with grey skies was not a good omen. He reversed out of his dilapidated shed of old sheets of tin and soon turned the corner towards Port Burnie. As he changed gears and tuned his radio, his spirits rose. He had to concentrate to see through his dirty windscreen and considered stopping to wash it when he saw Ned in his patrol car parked in the truck bay ahead.

'Hi, Ned. Just going to wash my windscreen so seeing you was good timing.' Secretly Bill knew if he was breathalysed, he'd be over the legal limit, despite the hour of the day. He busied himself with washing the windscreen as quickly as he could while Ned sat in his car drinking coffee freshly poured from his thermos.

When Ned saw it was Bill, he stepped from the car and offered him a towel to help with clearing the grime.

'Thanks, Ned. You're prepared for all occasions!' and he tried to move away from Ned before he could smell alcohol on his breath. Ned reached into the patrol car and took out his thermos and gave it to Bill. 'I think you could do with some of this,' and he poured coffee into a clean mug.

'Yep, thanks.' The silence between the two men was broken only occasionally by the noise of crows hanging around on the off-chance of food. No words were spoken for a while, both men knowing Bill would register on the breathalyser, and Bill aware of Ned's ever-watchful eyes on the coming and going of everyone's house in Carinya, including the house next to his. He would have seen John's car in the driveway late into the night.

Then Ned asked the question he'd been burning to ask for some time. 'How is Jane doing these days, mate?'

Bill shrugged nonchalantly. 'Slowing down,' he said bluntly.

Ned nodded. 'Her mind still sharp?' Ned prodded the point.

Bill nodded and surveyed Ned with narrowing eyes.

'That's good. It's just that I saw her some months back wandering round the town park, dithering. Seemed lost … I was just concerned, mate.'

Bill just nodded and the awkward moment ended, Bill soon flicking Ned a wave and driving away. In the rear vision mirror, Bill glimpsed Ned watching him until he was out of sight. If John had been in the car, he would have interpreted Ned's actions, or inactions, as a possibility for future blackmail, but Bill discounted the thought. Bill knew Ned knew he'd be over the legal limit, and so he didn't breathalyse him. This might have affected their relationship.

The truth was, Ned had sat waiting for Bill on the only exit from town. He'd intended to stop Bill on the pretence of saying goodbye and offering him a swig of coffee when it became apparent Bill had alcohol on his breath. He had no intention of bringing out the breathalyser – but he did get to ask his question about Jane. She had been in the park, acting weird, on edge.

Ned liked keeping tabs on folk. Who knew when information on them would come in handy. In the meantime, naive Bill would continue on his merry way, totally oblivious of Ned's plan. Police diary entries would be made.

Chapter 16

Jane Deteriorates

As the town of Port Burnie appeared in the distance, Bill decided to wait for his eldest son to arrive home. He couldn't quite face telling Jane about the sale of their family home, even though they'd both agreed to it, so he steered the Toyota Landcruiser towards Michael's place, driving very slowly.

As he sat in the car with the engine off and the radio on, he thought hard about the emotions involved in human behaviour and soon he felt himself nodding off. His head dropped back against the soft upholstery. With all the windows up, the car was warm, the sound of distant traffic soothing; it meant others, no matter how random, were nearby. Soon he'd be on his own and would be seeking the company of others for his own comfort. Jane being gone was a thought he could hardly bear, and he felt his eyes tear up just as he drifted into sleep. He assumed this was the beginning of grieving.

'Dad, what are you doing here?' Michael yelled sometime later.

The late afternoon sun was poking through the window when Bill lurched and realised he'd been sound asleep. He wound the window down as he shifted in his seat in a bid to become alert.

'Dad, go around to Donna's and be with Mum. Seriously, Dad, I don't think she's got long to go.'

By this time, the window was down, and Bill could see Mike had just finished work.

'I'll get cleaned up and bring around something to eat.'

Michael quickly walked down the path towards his back door and disappeared. He took off his boots and, as he looked up, he noticed lights on in his house. The kitchen was occupied and there, standing at the doorway, was his new girlfriend, Asha.

'Ahhhhhh, you don't know how pleased I am to see you. And I can smell something delicious coming my way.'

A nurse at the hospital with Donna, Asha's shift had finished at 3 o'clock. Michael had recently opened the discussion for Asha to move in with him and, smelling dinner, almost made him extend that information to something far more permanent. His heart beat strongly, and he realised where he'd been cautious not to rush into any long-term relationship, Asha was different. His caution had stemmed a lot from watching Ryan's issues with his girlfriends and then Jodie – all take and no give – and now all he had worked for was at risk. Some of Michael's girlfriends had been the same. But not Asha – she was generous to a fault, and had changed his attitude. If he wanted her in his life and not frighten her off, he had to be on his best behaviour; he couldn't be the slob around the house anymore; and he certainly couldn't flirt with the girls on the jetty.

'You can take this around to Donna's for your parents,' she said. 'I ate at the hospital and am on shift later, so I'll need to take a nap. Off you go now,' she purred.

Michael smiled inwardly, enjoying the most beautiful apparition he'd ever seen. Her long, curly brown hair hung around her face, framing her beauty, and accentuating her sensuous grey eyes. Michael determined that, if he played his cards right he could woo her into saying Yes, when the time was right, but it would need time. He still couldn't believe his luck that they'd met, he thought as he headed to the bathroom with clean clothes stuffed under his arms.

He let the warm shower water surround him and luxuriated in his new relationship as he washed his hair and enjoyed the smell of fresh soap. *Yep, Asha is a keeper. I'm real lucky. Pity about Ryan though. Jodie was such a waste of time ... and now she's disappeared ...? Perhaps he'll get lucky and find an angel for himself next time.* He sighed deeply. *Yeah, mate, you need to be kind to your brother right now; he's going through a rough time.* Eventually, he dried off and dressed and was ready to deliver dinner to his folks and Donna and Garry. And he needed to spend time with his mum.

***

The weeks unfolded and time stood still. 'Donna, you're a nurse! Poor Mum! How long does this go on?'

'Mike, I know you're at your wit's end, but sometimes this does last for weeks. Sometimes it's only days. Her breathing is laboured but she is holding on, lord knows why.'

Jane lay propped up on her pillows, the oxygen tube laying across her chest as she stared straight ahead, concentrating on taking her next breath.

'We need to keep her propped up, so her lungs drain. When the fluid reaches a certain level, she will find breathing even more difficult,' Donna added, her voice beginning to quiver.

The vital question of when that would happen prodded everyone's mind as the television in the lounge room moaned endlessly before they all went to bed.

Winter raged outside and the windows rattled in their panes, crying out for stillness but it wouldn't come. Occasionally, branches fell on rooftops, and rain pelted non-stop. Michael dozed off in the chair, trying to fill in time until he could leave without being rude. All he wanted to do was be with Asha, then he remembered she worked the late shift this week.

'Garry, Donna, I'm off home now. I won't disturb Dad'.

'Righto, Mike. See you next time,' Garry said, placing his jumper on the arm of the chair as he lifted himself up to speak with Michael. 'How's Ryan doing? He comes to see his mother but leaves quite quickly. I think all this Jodie business is dreadful for him and then Jane is so unwell. Not a good time for us.'

'I'll make a point of seeing him tomorrow. At least now winter's here, we can have the boat on dry dock for repairs. I want to chat with him about the future of the boat anyway.' Michael looked wistfully at his uncle. 'How's your business going?'

'Like yours. Winter is slow, but at least we don't have to worry about casual workers for a while, just doing the paperwork for the tax man. I'll see Steven soon too. Costs are going up so much that we won't have a big tax bill this year. One of the perks, I guess. Luckily, we aren't reliant on one income. We're probably both a bit lucky that people get sick and go to hospital. Just kidding!'

He smiled grimly. 'By the way, I reckon you've got a winner in Asha! She's kind and loving. I bet all the patients in the hospital love her. And I reckon you're just the slightest bit smitten?'

Michael laughed. 'Absolutely!' He felt good, and realised he hadn't laughed for some time. Asha was indeed a gem and made him feel good about himself. As he ambled outside and plodded along the path, avoiding puddles, deep down he realised he did actually love her. It was a word he was usually reluctant to use. And despite the rain and cold, he felt a warm glow surround him as he had that epiphany – He loved her!

He closed the door, turned the radio up loud and drove home recklessly, feeling invigorated by this newfound acceptance of his feelings. That night, he slept soundly, knowing she finished work late and would snuggle up beside him as morning greeted them.

***

As Michael opened the car door at Ryan's the next morning, he could smell the pungent aroma of burning rubbish from the neighbour's place. He tried to hold his breath to prevent inhaling the awful fumes that made him suddenly nauseous. 'Ryan! Ryan, are you home?' Michael called.

After some time, Ryan opened the door, looking like he'd just been woken up. 'Sorry, Mike. I had a rough night … awake for hours just rehashing everything, and then, near daylight, I finally went to sleep.'

He rubbed his eyes and ran his hand through his tussled hair. 'Come in. Come in out of the cold.' He held the door open. 'Thank goodness Emily is staying with a friend for a few days. Ultimately, she'll come home so I need to pull myself together.'

'You're right about that, mate. Life's tough. What more can I say?'

'The police think I did it, Mike! Can you believe that? They want to pin her disappearance on me.' He sank onto a chair and suddenly started sobbing. Michael gripped his shoulders and held him, his tight grip willing strength into his brother.

'I didn't do it, Mike. I didn't do anything to her!'

'Of course, you didn't! Ryan; we all know that. The Police are just doing their job. That's what they do. Because you're the husband of that nutter, and word was out she wanted a divorce, you're the first person they'd suspect.' Michael gave his brother's shoulders a squeeze and gentle shake. 'But, mate, you've got to pull yourself together. You are a suspect, but you're not guilty. And anyone who knew her would want to take her out!' He raised an eyebrow, quite high. '… if that is what's happened ….'

The brothers looked at each other, smiled, shook their heads and let normality reign. Gradually, Ryan calmed and, before long, he looked at Michael. 'You know, you're right!'

'Of course, I'm right. I'm always right. Honestly, bro, she needed to go. Whether she's run off or something's happened, it needed to happen.' He sighed deeply having blurted out his honesty. 'Now let's put the kettle and toaster on. I'm hungry.'

Soon the kettle was boiling, and Ryan made coffee for them both. 'Don't tell me I have to look after you as well as the folks,' Michael added.

Ryan didn't answer, just stepped forward and opened the window to let in the grey sky.

'For Christ's sake! Keep the cold out! It's freezing, man. What are you thinking? It's like you have a death wish. Put the kettle back on if you need to do something.'

Ryan followed his instructions in a daze.

'I'll send Dad over to look after you,' Michael said as Ryan passed him a cup. He'd been only half joking but, after a few moments, thought it would be a good idea. 'I'll sit with Mum.' He shivered. 'What a good thing we're not out on the boat. It's freezing and I'm glad we don't have contract commitments.' He aired his thoughts, almost to reassure himself as he watched his family fall apart. It wasn't really time to talk about new plans for the boat and their business. And it certainly wasn't time to reveal his new girlfriend on the scene.

***

'Dad, I think you'd better go and see Ryan. He's in a bad way at the moment, and paranoid the police will charge him over Jodie's disappearance. Honestly, that boy needs to calm down. They can't charge him with anything without any proof. Give him a few sensible ideas, can you, Dad?'

He put a hand on his father's thin bony shoulder as he passed behind him in Donna's kitchen. It was still early morning, but Michael wished he himself could feel calmer. This was going to be a long day and he'd need all the resources he could muster. Despite Bill's woolly jumper, his frailty was evident, and Michael realised time stood still for no man, even his poor father. So far, the attention had been on Jane but Bill was suffering too. This was taking a toll on him.

'Dad, off you go. I'll watch over Mum. I guess Donna and Garry have left for work?'

There was no answer for some time, then Bill said, 'The palliative care nurse, Ella, will be here soon. Mike, perhaps you could take care of all that, could you?' Bill looked tiredly towards Michael, who forced himself to brighten. He'd met and liked Ella and thought Ryan could do with a good dose of the cheerfulness Ella brought with her. Her bubbly personality and the way she bounced around was like a fairy from Wonderland. He'd also noticed the lack of a ring on her finger, had wondered about her life but didn't dare quiz her, except for information about his mum. Perhaps he could gauge the situation when Ella arrived, for later when the Jodie situation was over, as he didn't want to complicate their lives at the moment, or raise suspicions by having a possible relationship going on. He half shrugged. Once he would have taken a second look at Ella himself, but not now Asha had entered his life. *Ryan should come here and meet her,* but he knew that would not be possible, so he turned his focus back to the current situation.

Soon, Bill left and Michael was on his own with his mother. She was still propped up on pillows, hardly able to speak. Her eyes remained shut most of the time but she answered when Michael spoke to her and was surprisingly coherent. She didn't complain, but recently her food intake had diminished and each spoonful someone fed her was an effort to swallow.

Suddenly, the home phone rang so Michael took the call. It was Ella: she was unable to attend the house as an emergency at the hospital had arisen and she was needed. She would visit later in the day.

'Mum, the nurse is going to be late today,' Michael said loudly to ensure Jane could hear him.

'It's all right, Mike. I can hear you clearly, I just can't open my eyes.'

As Michael looked at his mother, his heart broke as he realised her time was close and a sob caught in his throat. He realised her personal needs wouldn't be met today and tomorrow seemed a long way off. He felt helpless, and holding her hand was all he could do. He gazed at the blankets under which lay her thin, skeletal form, and shook his head that she still had a beating heart. When he thought she had gone to sleep, he put his head against her arm and allowed himself to cry.

Chapter 17

The Passing of Jane

The sound of the ticking clock in the kitchen became obliterated by Jane's noisy breathing. *Is this the death rattle doctors told us about?* Michael froze ... *and now it's like a beating drum calling her.* He realised this sound had been present for some time but it hadn't registered in his consciousness. He stopped his own breathing and listened, feeling suddenly colder.

'Michael, ... are you ... still ... here?'

With bloodshot, puffy eyes, Michael looked at his mother and squeezed her hand lightly. 'Yes,' he whispered. 'I'm here. Is there anything I can do for you? Ella's coming later today to check your pain pump.'

'I'm so ... tired, ... Michael.' She could barely get the words out, her breathing so laboured. 'Please let me ... go. ... I wanna go.'

Michael wiped away a tear that trickled down the leathery skin that stretched under her eyes and over the bones of her cheeks, the moisture making a last-ditch effort at life. 'Please, Mike, ... turn off ... the oxygen tank like ... a good boy and ... let me go.'

Michael's jaw fell slack and his heart contracted as he realised the enormity of her request.

Her hand feebly indicated the ambulatory infusion pump on her shoulder. 'Leave this ... on. I'm ... begging you, Michael. *Please!* I can't keep ... up ... this charade. I just want to rest perm … anently. … I see the pain … in all your … faces. Let me go. Now. While there's … no one else around.'

Michael blinked away his own tears and tried to look at his mother. Her tears had all finished now and her eyes were shut tight. Her cracked, dry lips were pressed tight as well, and he was glad. He'd seen death before and it wasn't pretty. And now his beautiful mother was asking him to do it to her – one last favour! *How can I refuse, considering everything she's given me,* jarred in his mind. He shook his head, allowing himself one last minute to consider it as he heard the time on his watch tick over. He looked at the metal tap on the top of the oxygen cylinder. Stared at it. Then, wearily, he lifted himself out of his chair and kissed his mother's cheek, noting how cold she felt.

'I do this for you, Mum. You gave me life and now I obey your wishes, knowing it's what you want.' The words caught in his throat, and he wasn't sure if he'd articulated them or whether they'd remained unsaid. He felt gutted but knew what had to be done. He bent down, and with his fingers, turned the tap and stopped the oxygen flow.

'Turn it back … on … when I'm … gone,' Jane wheezed.

In moments, her breath began to labour more and became raspy. But she closed her eyes and looked peaceful even though the death rattle had started again. Each tortured breath Jane took seemed to last forever and Michael sat and buried his head in the blankets, put his hands over his ears and shut his eyes.

After a while, the room felt colder, and Michael removed his hands from his ears. His mother's noisy breathing had stopped, and he opened his eyes. He wasn't sure whether it was the sight of his still mother smiling or the lack of her breathing that registered first, but he clutched her hand in his and held it to his cheek as if trying to put warmth back into her. Then he buried his head against her and cried. He stayed like this for some time, then noticed that the cold had left the room. He looked at her and it seemed like he was looking at a stranger, and realised that his mother's soul had left the room. Then something prodded his mind. She had told him to do something. And wisely, he lifted the oxygen tube clear of her face and turned the oxygen back on.

All this happened in the morning.

Still shocked, he made a strong coffee and slathered it with cream. A feeble sun struggled to emerge from behind a cloud as Michael opened the back door and stood outside, trying to warm himself before summoning up the next lot of courage he needed to deal with this chaos. In time, he swallowed the last mouthful, reluctantly knowing he would need to face Death when he went inside.

It was silent and cold. In his mother's bedroom, she lay on the bed in a state of quiet repose, so he fluffed up her pillows to make her look more comfortable, and smoothed her hair, wondering how many times she'd completed the same actions when she was alive. Her hair had streaks of grey now invading her beautiful brown hair and it had been some time since she'd had it cut and styled. He allowed her head to rest on her chest, assuming the most natural pose possible, and knew an ambulance would need to be called at some stage, but he needed to speak with Ella first. She would know what to do.

He knew he also needed to pull himself together, and plan what to do and say. And he needed to think fast as the morning had not proceeded as he'd expected – he hadn't planned on ending a loved one's life and wondered when the shock of what he'd done would set in. This was like chapter two for the day, and he breathed deeply to keep his wits about him as he picked up the phone.

'Ella, can you please come around? It's happened.'

The dreaded phone call to the palliative care team made, he then rang Donna and his father.

Cockatoos shrieked in the trees as Michael waited outside for someone to come; it was like they were accusing him.

Donna pulled into the driveway first, followed by Bill. 'I knew I should have stayed home today,' she wailed as she rushed past him, letting the flywire door bang behind her. 'She was poorly last night … Michael, what happened?' But she didn't wait for an answer. Instead, she rushed to Jane's room, breathless.

'I guess we needed to prepare ourselves, son,' said Bill quietly as he strode towards Michael.

'Guess so, Dad. But it's still a shock when it happens.' Michael almost retched as the consequence of his actions dawned on him. 'I've rung Ella. She'll come around as soon as she can. Think I'd better sit down. I'm not feeling so good myself.'

Donna staggered from the bedroom. 'It's just different when it's someone you love or someone you know. Dealing with deceased who are unknown is so much easier … you keep your distance. But this … … …'

She turned away, grappling with her emotions. 'You both might want to see Jane before Ella gets here. I'd go in now if I was you.'

As Michael stood in the doorway, his eyes were drawn to the oxygen cylinder. It was still switched on and Michael froze. His fingerprints were on it … *What if someone suspects something?* A cold chill washed over him and he stayed focused on the 'what ifs'. Then he snapped out of it as a plan fixed in his head.

'Dad, you sit with Mum, and I don't think she needs this on any longer,' he said as he nonchalantly moved forward and turned off the cylinder tap. His fingerprints now had a reason for being there, and he had a witness.

Bill only had eyes for Jane and sat looking down at her lovingly. So many years together had come down to this.

Seeing him like that churned Michael's gut. 'Donna, I'm feeling pretty rough right now. I'm going home for a while. Guess you're able to deal with Ella when she comes?'

The blood left Michael's face and he couldn't even look at his aunt. His face ashen, he ran a hand over his mouth and chin and realised he needed a shave and a freshen-up.

'You really should be here when Ella arrives,' Donna said as he reached the verandah.

He looked at the ground as his tears filled his eyes. 'I'll be back,' he muttered, his heart breaking as he stumbled to his car and sat in the warmth. *Donna's right. I'm the last person to see Mum alive and someone from the hospital will want to talk me. So pull yourself together!* Slowly he opened his car door again and went back inside.

'Mike, it's all right. Ella's on her way. I can deal with her if you need time to compose yourself.' She gave him a tight hug, and Michael felt his whole body relax. He slumped into the nearest chair where he remained for some time.

Before long, Ella's face appeared at the doorway. 'Hello. Can I come in?' She offered her condolences to everyone with a hug as she slowly and knowingly made her way towards Jane's room, Donna close behind her.

'Donna, guess you know what to do now. You would have done this before. Let's just remove the oxygen tube and bottle, and I'll disconnect the Pain Pump and return them to the hospital. We'll leave Jane so family can say their goodbyes, then we'll need to arrange for the Death Certificate and you can call the Funeral Service.'

Michael realised how routine the procedure was for medicos. 'Michael, can you ring Doctor Baker and let him know what's happened? He'll come around soonish, I guess.

We'll take care of the necessary tasks with Jane once we get all this gear away.'

Donna, too, had slipped into work mode and Mike stood with his father as the procedure unfolded before them.

'It looks so procedural, Dad, doesn't it?' But Bill couldn't speak.

In the quietness of the kitchen, Donna turned to Mike. 'Mike, because it's a death at home, the police and coroner will become involved. That's just how it plays out. Even though we knew it was inevitable, it's still a shock for us all,' Donna said in hushed tones, which pacified Michael, who had now gained control of his nerves.

Jane's body looked so peaceful, and Michael was thankful Donna had medical training. He guessed Asha would deal with these situations too.

Ryan and Emily arrived and, though distraught, were pleased Jane looked so peaceful.

Ultimately, the ambulance arrived, and they all watched as Jane was respectfully taken away. Numbness then set in as each family member was embroiled in their own private thoughts.

Later, the police arrived and were sympathetic as they spoke with Michael and Donna.

***

In the busy days afterwards, Michael and Donna had a chance to talk. 'I'm glad you rescued your mother, Mike,' Donna said soon after Jane's passing. 'She didn't want to drag it out, with the pain and anxiety that accompanies death. She told me once she didn't want to get sick and look horrible. She didn't want to experience the deterioration of the mind that accompanies the body's decline so, Mike, you spared her of all that. You saved her from further misery and I want you to remember her in good times. She was deteriorating fast when she passed away and she would thank you for what you did.'

Michael's jaw set as her words hung around him. He couldn't meet her eyes initially but then looked straight at her. 'What makes you think I had anything to do with it?' he said, resenting her accusation, her knowledge.

Donna looked straight back at him, certainty in her eyes. 'Because she asked me to do it … but I couldn't. I loved her, but I couldn't.'

Michael couldn't look at her.

'I suspected she would ask you next – she knew Bill couldn't do it. You were the strong one.'

Now he had the courage to look up. But he didn't admit to anything. He never would.

'Although her body has gone, you and I know her spirit will live on in us all. It sounds cliched, but she left beautiful memories which is all any of us could want.'

Michael muttered a few words and thoughts invaded his mind, but his eyes felt hot and dry as he tried to smile at the woman who knew his mother better than anyone. She was on his side, if taking sides was on the agenda, and Michael felt a wave of relief sweep over him, yet he hated himself for what he'd done, regardless of what Donna had said.

***

Donna never referred to that conversation again, and Michael was left to deal with his conundrum and the accompanying demons. Regularly at night he remembered Donna's words and felt reassured, despite having committed murder. Slowly, and with the help of Asha's embraces, he coped with the grief accompanying his mother's death, though not a word passed between any family members. In his mind, as the eldest child, he needed to look after all of the family.

Chapter 18

The Return of Lexie and Talia

The walls of the Carinya town hall were squeezed to capacity as Jane's wake unfolded. Eulogies were delivered, words spoken, and photos displayed in a slide show during the funeral service.

'I'm so pleased you were here to farewell Jane,' Donna said quietly to Talia and Lexie.

'Mum, as soon as we knew Aunty Jane was in palliative care, we made plans to return. We'll stay a while too. We've both taken indefinite leave, so here we are.'

Just like in old times, Lexie spoke for her sister. It had become natural, as Lexie, the eldest, assumed a leadership role and her sister naturally followed. *Nothing's changed*, thought Donna as she looked at her daughters and then moved away to mingle with the crowd, which was customary on such occasions. Condolences were muttered and accepted by all the family members. All the cousins, who normally gathered at Christmas, mixed easily with the inhabitants of Carinya. Being a country funeral, all the townsfolk attended to pay their respects.

Lexie sipped her tea and, scanning the crowd, saw Donna talking to Fay and John.

'Talia, why do you think the family is friendly with John and Fay? I could never work out the connection and what they do.'

Talia followed Lexie's gaze and caught a glimpse of them in the crowd. 'I heard someone say they work for the government, but from home. And that's highly unusual. All I know is they were Aunty Jane's best friends. Oh well, from my limited experience of the world, nothing is ever as it seems. Perhaps they're spies!' The sisters giggled covertly, then Lexie forced her gaze away from John and Fay, acutely aware she didn't want to be caught staring. The girls mingled with the crowd, never far away from each other.

'Let's look for Ryan. I haven't seen him since we left the cemetery. I'm sure he's here somewhere,' Talia suggested.

They scanned the crowd, fixed expressions on their faces, as they finished their tea. Talia gathered up other empty cups and returned them to the centre table, where others offered condolences as they stood and made small talk. Soon, they saw Garry and when they asked about Ryan, he looked concerned.

'To tell the truth, I'm a bit worried about him. He's got a lot on his plate with Jodie's disappearance. Now with the funeral to cope with … he's probably gone home.' Garry sighed and looked at the girls; they stared back at him.

'Surely he wouldn't leave without telling you?' Lexie replied, frowning. 'And you did drive here together, didn't you?' Garry mumbled something under his breath and scanned the crowd, which was gradually starting to leave. Lexie continued. 'Look, why don't Talia and I go back to his place and we'll ring you when we catch up with him.'

Garry sighed with relief and nodded. 'Don't forget to leave your phone off silent and leave it where you can hear it ring.'

***

'Honestly, old people and their phones,' said Talia as she and Lexie drove towards Port Burnie. 'I'll give Ryan a call now.' She dialled and sighed as she waited for a response. 'Still not answering. Come on, Ryan, answer your phone.'

Lexie felt a dull ache as she listened to Talia and then accelerated, almost as though she had a sixth sense about her cousin. He always had his phone on him and now he wasn't answering! She felt overwhelmed with the range of possibilities and tried to resist the impulse to speed – she knew the local traffic cop, who may or may not have been at the wake, had a habit of waiting for easy targets on the road out of Carinya. Instead, she turned the music up and focused on the radio, hoping Talia wouldn't interrupt by voicing her concerns.

All too soon, Ryan's house came into view and Lexie turned her head towards the bungalow at the end of the street. It needed a lot of maintenance – actually, it looked terribly unloved. She skidded the car to a halt, shut the door noisily then struggled with the iron gate that was meant to be locked. Hurrying along the pathway, leaving Talia to come behind her, she noticed the shed door was open and entered.

Ryan was busy at his workbench, attending to a rope. Another rope had been slung across a rafter beneath the roof and a chair had been placed beneath it. Lexie froze. And her eyes widened when she realised Ryan hadn't seen her. He was so intent on what he was doing at the bench. She looked around the shed and then back at Ryan, as Talia entered through the door, and stood behind her.

'Ryan!' she screamed. 'What the hell do you think you're doing!' She heard Talia gasp behind her. 'Ryan, what are you doing?' she screamed again. 'Stop it! Stop it!' She could hear the hysteria in her voice as she moved towards him.

Then Ryan turned his head and saw her; he spun around, absolute shock on his face. Then it changed to ferocity and he lurched forward and screamed at her. 'WHAT ARE YOU DOING HERE? GET OUT!!' He ran at them, went to push

Lexie who stood her ground and pushed him away. Then he started ranting, like a wild animal, caged and stressed. It seemed to go on for an eternity. Then he dropped to his knees, sobbing, yet still screaming, with the intensity of a man beaten.

'What are you doing here? Who asked you here?' he screamed between rants and sobs. 'Go away.'

'Talia, call an ambulance quickly,' Lexie yelled without turning around. 'Call one now!'

'No, no, don't do that. *Please … ….*'

Slowly, Ryan's sobbing decreased, and time stood still, for a long time.

***

Later, in the kitchen, Ryan sat mute, his tears finally exhausted.

'Ryan, what were you thinking? Honestly!! You couldn't possibly think about topping yourself!'

'Talia, a little bit of sensitivity now would be helpful,' Lexie warned, glaring at her sister.

Ryan ignored them both, but Lexie realised the threat of an ambulance had finally brought Ryan to his senses.

'Talia, perhaps you could go to the shed and um … ….'

Talia nodded. 'Sure.' She didn't need to be told twice and she certainly wanted to disband the whole suicide sight that had been playing out in front of them. For her, she wanted to get out of the kitchen and leave Ryan in Lexie's care. Her legs felt shaky as she left the house, her heart still racing. Her stomach twisted tightly, and she felt like throwing up as saliva flooded her mouth. She felt lightheaded and faint, but slowly, as she walked into the fresh air, she gradually recovered and sank onto the back lawn to rest, the wetness of the lawn seeping into her trousers.

Rain still clung to clouds, threatening to fall as the black clouds reinforced the seriousness of the situation. Unsure of what was expected to do exactly to 'clear up' the shed, she shifted a few items around and brought the chair outside onto the verandah.

Emboldened by her new role as 'rescuer', Lexie put mugs of tea onto the kitchen table and initiated the conversation. 'Ryan, do you know if we'd called an ambulance, the mental health care team would come on board and administer all kinds of risk assessments on you? It would severely impact your work. You would be deemed unsuitable for the responsibility of a crew at sea. The consequences of an accident and the litigation which would follow would be unbelievably traumatic.'

Silence hung loud in the room, only interrupted by the purring of the fridge. The awkwardness of the situation hung around like the rope in the shed. Ryan wrung his hands together and looked devastated, maybe even shocked at his own intentions.

'You've had a bad experience but what you've attempted would be absolutely dreadful for the family.' She paused to let her words sink in. 'What about Emily? Who do you think would find you?'

Voices from neighbours next door penetrated the tension in the room and, finally, Ryan's sniffles lessened.

'The cops think I did it! They keep asking all these questions and all I can see is my life in jail,' Ryan stammered gruffly with an intensity to shock all in the room. He cupped the mug as if to steady his hands as the knowledge of his actions began to sink in. 'I can't see beyond it. Nothing else matters.' Then he pushed the mug away and let his head sink into his arms on the table.

'Ryan! What about Emily? What about your dad?' Talia demanded, the angst in her voice barely disguised. 'How could you?' The strain in her voice bit at Ryan hard. 'The cops are just doing their job. With you and Jodie having marital issues, what would you expect? Word gets around. They'd know your situation. I reckon, you don't tell anyone about this.'

She took a deep breath. 'You need to pull yourself together, Ryan. Of course, you're going to be questioned! And now with an attempted suicide, they would definitely think you are guilty and diagnose you with mental health issues and say that's why you did it!'

'Keep quiet, Talia. No one's saying anything to anyone. Do we all understand?' Lexie sounded like a stranger, even to herself, and she realised her own wrath was barely concealed.

Ryan lifted his tear-stained face and glared at the girls. Then he started shouting again as he rose from his chair. 'You don't know what it's like to have nightmares all night. Every night. Then I can't sleep and then I don't want to be here!' He turned suddenly and kicked the chair away as he stormed from the room. The sisters looked on helplessly, each wanting to comfort him but not knowing what to do next.

***

Later in the afternoon, Garry answered his phone. 'What's up, kiddo? I'm in the car with Donna and Emily.'

'Hiya, Garry. Can you call me back when you've got a spare moment?' Thankful she had heard Emily was in the car, Lexie breathed with relief – there was no way she needed to hear the state her father was in. Lexie was most relieved to end the call.

Soon enough, Garry was in a position to call.

'You need to keep Emily with you and Donna. Ryan's had a breakdown and she doesn't need to see him like this. Talia and I will stay with Ryan. I'll give you the details later but, right now, we need to be vigilant.'

When Emily was asleep in her room, Garry and Donna discussed the day's events. 'I'm pleased Michael and Bill agreed to stay the night in Carinya. Such a big day and so many people. So hard to keep up cheerfulness when I just want to say how unfair it is to lose Jane before she even turns 70.'

Garry turned towards Donna and read the strain on her face. The beginning of grey hairs just peeped around the edges of her face and one or two lines had made their appearance around her beautiful blue eyes. The week before the funeral had been frenzied, and Donna felt emotionally exhausted and found maintaining the façade emotionally draining. She felt pleased to be home in her own space and had decided not to work for the rest of the week. She put her feet up on the footstool in the lounge room and let the television drone on just loud enough to ensure she and Garry could hear each other talking.

Through the open window, the smell of winter moisture drifted in and with it came the cool damp air, so Donna closed it and dismissed the outside sounds and smells. She put the kettle on for a hot chocolate drink which began their night-time ritual, an important part of Donna's routine.

Just then, the phone rang, and Donna felt relieved Garry took the call in the office. She soon identified the caller as Lexie and was curious to know what had happened to Ryan.

'Well, looks like Emily will be with us for a few days,' Garry told her. 'Lexie and Talia will stay at Ryan's. Apparently, he's had a huge meltdown, whatever that means. But for us, it means Emily is here and our girls are elsewhere.'

Chapter 19

The House Becomes Ned's

Bill returned to his home of many years exhausted, the wake in Carinya taking its toll. He stood looking at the home where they'd lived since selling the farm and shook his head as memories crowded in. Someone at the funeral had told him not to look back; he needed to look forward. So, that night he read his book until his eyes could stay open no longer and then he fell into a deep and fitful sleep, waking the next morning feeling guilty that he'd slept so well.

After his toast and coffee, he began the arduous job of packing. He needed to be ruthless this time, and thankfully, Michael woke early and was ready to help his father pack.

'Dad, chuck this out.'

Bill cleared his throat before mumbling a non-committed response, meant to placate him. Someone had left packing boxes for them at the front door, which was indicative of the nature of small county towns. Some generous person had recognised a need and donated the boxes, so gradually a box was allocated to each room and filled.

Eventually, Michael said, 'Dad, let's go to the pub for lunch. I'm buggered and I know you must be too.'

Bill looked up and nodded wordlessly.

'We'll see Colleen to finalise the paperwork for your deal with Ned, and I reckon by the end of the week, we'll leave here with your stuff and Ned can have access to the place,' he added.

Bill nodded again. 'I knew we had a great son for a reason,' and they both laughed as they ambled along the uneven path to the car.

'Another thing, Dad. You'll have a nice fat bank balance, too, by the time we leave. A new beginning for you, Dad, just you wait and see.'

***

Ned peeped through the sheer kitchen curtains as he finished crunching on his toast, and noted the packing boxes on the front step. A while later, he squinted and stared hard, absently wiped egg yolk off his face as he registered the boxes were now gone and assumed Michael and Bill were packing. Even later, he decided to drive around in the squad car to keep an eye on their whereabouts. He suspected the townsfolk referred to him as Nosey Ned, and if they did, they had good reason to, he smirked.

Soon, the men left the pub and drove around to Colleen's. Ned decided to hang around outside his car in case he could glean snippets of conversation through the open front window. While in uniform, he could register his snooping as 'being on the job' and he couldn't help smiling inwardly and outwardly. Obviously, Bill and Michael were organising the house hand-over so he could expect a withdrawal from his bank account soon. Other people may be dismayed by their bank balance heading south but, for him, it was a new beginning, or rather, a focus on something different. The next stage for him was to resign from the Police Force and organise his superannuation. Cash payments from other debts owing to him would happen as Ned planned. He could almost hear gold coins jingling in his

141

pocket. *And God help anyone who doesn't pay up when their debts are due!*

As Michael and Bill left Colleen's, Michael's phone vibrated in his back pocket. 'Hang on, Dad. It's Garry. I'd better take it. Do you want to wait in the car?'

Bill nodded, glad to be out of the cold winter wind, and headed up the street towards Michael's vehicle.

'So, what's up, Garry?' The cold July wind blew around Michael as he moved further down the street away from the car and pulled his jumper tightly across his chest. He wished he'd worn a beanie as his ears were cold and his eyes were watering. He continued walking back and forth in the hope Garry would be brief so he could enjoy the warmth in the car with his dad. 'Dad's just on his way to the car so I'm on my own, but it's freezing out here. This wind's straight off the South Pole.'

'Righto, I'll be brief,' Garry assured him. 'When you return, you need Bill to stay with you for a bit. Emily is staying here with us as Ryan's had a meltdown. I'll talk to you later about what happened, but it's all somewhat mysterious and Lexie and Talia are saying very little. They told me Ryan was upset and they would stay with him until the end of the month.'

Michael sighed inwardly and he reflected on Ryan's lack of mental strength. He was never good in an emergency and now he was wimping out as soon as the pressure was on.

'No worries,' he said. 'I get the drift. Those girls will do a great job with Ryan. You and Donna handle Emily. And yes, I think I got the easy job! Dad can stay with me until he finds himself somewhere to live.'

'How's the packing, or I should say the throwing out, going?'

'Look, it's progressing as expected. We've just sorted out the paperwork so Ned Lawson can pay the deposit so we'll have most of the stuff out of the house by the end of the week. He's just leaving enough comfort stuff in case he wants to stay over when visiting friends.' Michael shivered. 'Look, mate, it's freezing here on the street. I'll call you when I have other news. Thanks for your call. I'd better keep Dad moving on the packing and get him out of this cold air. Talk to you later.'

Michael clicked his phone off, replaced it in his back pocket and looked around for his father. Near the corner, he could see Bill talking to Ned. He didn't feel like talking to Ned so he decided to walk on past and get the engine idling, so Bill could climb in when he took his leave from the local cop.

***

Later, when driving back to the house, Michael said, 'Dad, don't tell Ned anything he doesn't need to know. He should deal with Colleen now, not you. Honestly, the less said, the better.'

Bill raised his eyebrows and looked up in surprise. 'You're not the first person to tell me to watch Nosey Ned,' he replied. He waited but no more was said on the matter, and the silence stretched out as Michael kept his eyes on the road until they reached the house.

Watching his father alight from the car, Michael noted his curved back and lanky arms. From all the years of manual work, Bill had acquired large hands and the years had ensured his neck was skinny with loose skin hanging on and fighting gravity. Sparse few hairs covered his scalp and his eyes seemed regularly watery. He was strong, but in recent times, the furrow in his brow had become permanent, which was not surprising given what he'd just dealt with. And he now moved awkwardly. Michael felt an ache invade his chest and then contract with grief. He hoped Death wouldn't catch his dad any time soon. It was bad enough losing one parent but the thought of losing them both was unbearable. He took a moment to contemplate his situation before closing the car door and making his way to the house.

'I don't know why I locked it,' Michael muttered as he struggled with the key. 'Who's going to break in? Dad, I reckon one of the first jobs old Ned will do is make the back door more secure.'

Eventually, the key found its happy spot in the lock and turned readily, allowing the men to enter and continue packing. 'But, son, I wonder how much Ned cares? We've got a few spare keys for doors and windows hidden away in different places in the garden.'

***

But Ned did care. He cared a lot about security, and he'd seen Michael struggle with the key and made a mental note to attend to such matters as soon as he moved in.

***

Time seemed to creep along slowly, with the coldness being an uninvited enemy in the Thompson family home, but all too soon, it was Saturday, the day the house became shared with someone else.

'Don't look back, Dad,' said Michael as he struggled to keep his own voice even. But Bill had run out of words and his thoughts were of Jane and their life in Carinya. He didn't want to leave Jane in the pine box out at the cemetery, but he knew he had to keep busy to avoid imagining what she must look like as the weeks unfolded and as Time wreaked havoc with the processes of nature deep in the ground.

Bill took his phone out in a frenzy and rang Garry. 'Gaz, can you give me some work as soon as you can? The friggin' demons are getting to me and I need to stay active.'

'Sure thing, Bill. Leave it with me,' Garry replied, not surprised to hear from Bill. He shrugged and gave a tight laugh. There could be as much work as Bill wanted. This was a good sign.

The humming noise from Michael's Toyota engine gradually became a comfort as Carinya became a blur in the rear vision mirror. The sky, with its black clouds, loomed large across the horizon. The car heating warmed the men and the minutes ticked past in a way that was comforting, each man locked in his own private thoughts. Michael had been rehearsing a speech for his father to inform him about Asha and his new domestic arrangements. He needed to broach it at the right moment to avoid him fleeing somewhere else, so Michael had been referring to Asha only so often during the last few days. But he really needed to reveal the facts sometime soon; it might as well be while they were driving.

'Well, I'll be damned! Is that old Nosey Ned out here on the road?' Michael checked his speedo, and eased his foot off the accelerator. 'And what's that black dot coming towards us? Looks like bikies. And there's quite a few of them.'

Michael slowed down and the bikies rode past nonchalantly, like they owned the road. 'And there are some more up there with a cop car.'

Within moments Ned stepped out onto the road and waved Michael past, the message clear: Do Not Stop! Michael made a small noise in his throat. 'A meeting place, no doubt.'

Bill turned towards his son, puzzled.

'Don't trust him, Dad. He's probably organising deals.' He cleared his throat. 'Dad, I need to let you know … I have a girlfriend who lives with me,' he literally blurted out.

Bill had been resting his eyes for a moment and wondered if he'd heard correctly. He delicately stopped himself from saying anything and waited for Michael to continue. Then he turned and looked at Michael before opening his mouth.

'Well, son, that's good.' It sounded so pedestrian and understated but this was new territory for Bill. He didn't know what else to say so he said nothing.

'I'm looking forward to introducing you to her. She's amazing, Dad. And she's an important part of my life, though I haven't introduced her as my girlfriend to anyone yet.'

'Then I'm privileged to be the first family member to meet her.' Bill's eyelids felt heavy, but he knew he needed to make an effort with this news. He looked out the window at the first sign of yellow from the canola crop, noting the flowers breaking through, and he saw a vehicle assuming its business, thus creating a sense of normality amidst this surreal moment. He wound his window down, just a touch, to lift the weight from his shoulders. The traffic intensified and soon they were approaching the place where Asha now lived – Michael's house.

'God, it's been a long day, son.'

The loneliness that had enveloped him for the past few months felt like it was releasing its grip, and, as Bill uncurled himself from the vehicle, he had a spring in his step. He made his way forward to meet one new female family member and slightly, just ever so slightly, let another one go.

Chapter 20

Change is in the Air

Talia and Lexie clicked their seat belts and prepared for the long flight to England. They hadn't intended Manchester to become their new home, nor move away from South Australia and all the family, but somehow, over the years, they'd become entrenched in their work: Talia as a flight attendant, and Lexie had recently purchased a veterinary practice, so being British citizens underpinned their lives.

'We could move back I suppose,' said Lexie. They settled into their seats as the plane began the humming that indicated the immediacy of take-off.

'No, we couldn't. And besides we don't want to. I like our lives just the way they are.'

They half-watched the staff attendant delivering the safety routine as the engine noise increased. 'We both love our jobs and flying home once a year suits me just fine.' They opened the plastic wrapping and unwound their headphones.

'Do you think we should fly home for Christmas?' Lexie asked as she opened her laptop, ready for a long viewing session.

'Well, when I said our goodbyes to Ryan, I told him we'd see him at Christmas. It's six months away so time will pass quickly. We just have to tighten our belts to afford it.'

Talia closed her eyes and remembered her time with Ryan. It had been such a shock to realise his predicament. What else could she say? She needed to give him some timeline to cheer him up and so much could happen in six months.

***

Ryan had been sorry to see his cousins depart and knew he'd miss their company. However, as time passed, he could see the error of his actions; he needed to be a proper father for Emily, who was still living with Donna and Garry. He sat at the kitchen table eating his toast, waiting for the kettle to boil. He had accounts to pay, so he started getting all his paperwork completed before Mike arrived after lunch. *It's no good procrastinating,* he thought, so he turned his phone off to avoid distractions and began the arduous task. The household accounts were one thing but preparing his mind for the boat work, which needed to be done, was quite another.

He sighed with relief when the side gate clicked and he recognised Mike's heavy steps coming along the wet path. He hoped Mike would wipe his feet before bringing mud onto his freshly washed floor. Talia and Lexie had cleaned his house and told him to prepare a home for Emily. *And they are firm and correct,* thought Ryan, *and it's just what I need. Now I don't need a brother who's not only bossy but oblivious to details like a clean floor.*

'Wipe your feet on the mat,' he called out.

'That's a great welcome, but never mind, I'll cut you some slack.'

Michael hadn't intended referring to his brother's recent suicide attempt, but his curtness always caught him by surprise, and his reply had slipped out before he could filter the words. He let the door close as quietly as possible and sat down.

'Look, Ryan, I'm going to get straight to the point and talk business.' *Ryan needs to toughen up and make better decisions,* Michael thought, *and I'm not prepared to babysit him anymore.* He drew a deep breath, *but talk calmly*. He sat at the end of the table away from Ryan's pieces of paper and his computer. 'I think we need to rethink what we do with the boat.' He leant back in his chair, crossed his arms and stared straight ahead.

'Nice work,' replied Ryan coolly. 'What do you suggest we do? I guess you've organised the anti-fouling and the boat to go up the slipway, or do you think we need a hydraulic lift? Surely old Don will talk about it with you when you see him.'

'Ah yeah, all that's taken care of.'

'Well, what new equipment do we need to buy?'

Michael pushed his chair out from the table and leant forward again. 'You don't mind if I make myself a coffee, do you?' He took a piece of paper from his pocket as he passed Ryan and went into the kitchen. The hum of the kettle provided a background noise and broke the strained silence.

'Look at this …' Michael took a deep breath and placed his sheet of paper in front of Ryan. 'I reckon we should convert the boat from a fishing boat into a glass bottom boat for tourists.' Michael made his coffee, giving Ryan the space to absorb his radical idea about the boat reconstruction. The minutes marched by as Ryan studied the picture of the glass bottom boat.

'Far out, Mike! That's radical.' The thin piece of paper fluttered to the floor as Michael passed by heading to the bench so he bent down, retrieved it and placed it on the table amongst all the other sheets of paper.

'Here, let me look at it again!' Ryan smoothed over the paper several times, like he was stroking it. 'I reckon that's a brain wave, mate.' A genuine smile crept across Ryan's face as he focused on the photo. 'It's certainly an idea with merit. Have you given it a lot of thought, or is it just an idea?'

'Bro, I've given this a lot of thought, but we both need to endorse the whole concept. I reckon it could be a goer.' Michael sipped his coffee.

'Shall we ask Dad if he would like to come in with us? I assume there will be quite a bit of expense.'

Michael put down his cup. 'Nah, I've thought about it, but I reckon Dad's got enough to deal with right now. He needs to buy a house and sort out Mum's Will. Not sure how long all that stuff's going to take. But let's count him out for now. Perhaps later we could see how he's travelling.'

Opening the fridge to get the milk, he was pleased that it contained lots of food. 'Good thing Lexie and Talia stayed here,' and he took a cooked chicken and some tomatoes from the shelf in the fridge and put food on two plates while Ryan continued to stare at the picture.

Both men ate hungrily as they realised eating provided a good distraction from the important life-changing decision that needed to be made. 'I guess this will require extra funds?' Ryan forced the words out through a mouthful of food.

'Look, let's not worry about that aspect of it quite yet. The main thing is that you endorse the idea.'

'Mike, yes. *Bring it on!*' Ryan felt lightheaded and realised how upset he'd been since Jodie disappeared. This would provide a much-needed distraction if nothing else. 'I need a new project.'

'Of course, you do. We both do.'

Now the decision had been made, talk came easily. From the corner of his eye, Michael glimpsed the cat emerging from a doorway and moving towards the kitchen.

'Hell, she's smelt the chicken. Give her the bones, Mike,' Ryan called. 'And grab a few beers out of the fridge. I think we need to celebrate our good idea.'

Michael picked up on the 'our' idea, but he didn't care. Ryan liked the notion, and he could see a change in the air. His long face softened and suddenly he realised what a strain the whole family had endured since his mother's death. It was now time for Emily to return home and try to live a life in Jodie's shadow.

'Bugger Jodie, and bugger the cops,' Ryan griped when Michael asked if he'd heard any news. 'Look, Mike, you go and investigate the glass bottom boat and I'll clear up this mess on the table before Emily comes home. Donna will bring her here for dinner tonight, so I must be fit enough to cook.' He began to feel it might be possible to continue living a normal life, and a sense of relief flooded over him. His life had been suspended and he'd felt like he was drowning under the weight of people and their expectations, but now the shore was within sight.

Michael also felt uplifted as he left his brother's home, knowing Emily's return was imminent. Concern over Jodie's disappearance was fading, and Ryan was learning to live with no knowledge of her whereabouts as best he could and relax in a kind of comfort he hadn't anticipated. He was back in the land of the living, and Michael was relieved. He just didn't want Jodie turning up and ruining that.

Before going to the marina, Michael decided to call his father to see how his house hunting was progressing, but his phone rang out, so Michael wasn't sure if he was looking at houses or simply organising his storage. His dad had set up a bed in the shed where all his boxes from Carinya had been dumped by the truck driver. His father's stoicism had surprised him but he figured his father had had time to adjust to his mother's passing. This was a new life for them all.

A thin drizzle had started falling by the time Michael arrived home, and he remembered Asha was working a late shift. He quite liked having the house to himself at times and felt sure Bill actually enjoyed his 'shed time' too.

'Gosh, Dad, perhaps we could set up a television for you out there.' Bill already had a fridge containing food.

'Not a bad idea, son, but by the time you do it, I'll have a new place to call home.' Bill stood in the wide doorway of the shed, the heater behind him creating a warm space. 'Gotta shut the door to keep the place warm,' he said, and so he strode with Michael towards the back verandah. He was cosy in Michael's shed and was more than content to give Michael some privacy with Asha. He had met and liked the girl, and hoped something permanent would eventuate.

'I needed to go to the pub this afternoon,' Michael said quietly to his father. 'I need to let Luke know I don't want any more drugs, of any sort. I'm on the square now.' Michael had suspected his dad knew about his drug habit, so a frank conversation now his mother wasn't around was the best way to go.

'Does Asha know?'

'Hell, no, Dad! That's why I had to stop as soon as I could. All finished now.' Yet Michael knew he sounded more confident than he felt. He also realised Luke wouldn't be too happy losing a customer. He felt slightly unsettled and tried to dismiss the likely smirk of dissatisfaction on Luke's face, and pushed the thought away that night as he prepared a meal for three on the gas stove. The smells of meat cooking always created a calming effect, and they enjoyed a meal of fatty meat and gravy, saving the vegetables for Asha. When the dishes were washed and dried, Bill opened a folder and showed Michael a photo of a house he'd found that day.

'What a bombshell of a day I've had, Dad! First Ryan and then you!' Michael exclaimed as he plopped into a lounge chair ready to hear a detailed description of some place his dad might or might not buy.

'Mike, I think I might put in an offer for this place. Luckily, it's nice and close. Not sure how you feel about your old man living a few streets away,' Bill chuckled.

'Now I can see you're serious, I'll pay attention,' Michael joked. 'Righto then, when shall we go and see it?'

'I've made an appointment with the agent for an inspection tomorrow afternoon. That'll give you time to do whatever you need to do in the morning and then we can go after lunch. What do you say?'

'Excellent,' and his thoughts quickly shifted to the sleep-in he'd planned for the morning. When Asha worked late shifts, the bonus was sleeping in together. 'Later in the day sounds spot on. Asha and I have a few things to do in the morning so I'll knock on your door then we can have a cuppa together.'

If Michael had anything to do with it, the next morning would be quite late when he knocked on the shed door! He had quite a spring in his step as he took out the rubbish and began his night-time ritual, which included warming up the bed for Asha. He particularly liked it when she brought the dinner he'd cooked to bed so they could talk about trivialities before retiring for the night. As he went through his routine, he reflected on all the changes in the air. *Today has been eventful for the Thompson family,* he thought as he shut all the windows tight to keep out the cold and dark.

Chapter 21

Bill's New Ventures

The next afternoon, as Michael stood by the car waiting for his father, the sun struggled vainly to come through the clouds. As the cool southerly wind intruded through his clothing, he thrust his hands in his pockets to keep them warm. The glass bottom boat still bobbed around in his mind, so much so his father's wish to buy a house was barely a distraction. He tried to focus on the latter as his father needed him right now and he wasn't going to undermine his excitement by overwhelming his dad with ideas of a glass bottom boat. His father may not even like the idea of them moving away from fishing and into the uncertain area of tourism.

'Sorry to keep you waiting,' Bill called as he came through the gate and strode towards the car.

'No worries, Dad,' Michael replied, waving a dismissive hand. 'In you hop!'

Bill gave him directions to the house around the corner, a blue asbestos house with an iron roof and a white picket fence. 'Love the fence, Dad.'

The house looked old, but when the agent let them in through the front door, Michael was pleasantly surprised that it had been recently renovated; it felt surprisingly warm and loved. The inside reminded Michael of their old home in Carinya and he could see why his father had chosen it. It would have reminded him of Jane as a young wife and mother. Even the garden looked similar, and Michael smiled inwardly. *Of course, Dad will buy this house.* He nodded, but a million questions ran through his head, and he knew the heart was more important than the head at this time, *so who cares if white ants are present or whether the plumbing's in order!*

Suddenly, a loud clattering came from outside, and they made their way to investigate. There, next to the back door, hung a bird cage housing a pink and white galah. 'The owners will take the bird with them,' the agent said, which Bill looked slightly disappointed about, but Michael was relieved. He wasn't too keen on birds as they made a racket, needed feeding, and attracted vermin. *This house is looking better by the minute!* The décor, too, looked familiar; in fact it looked so familiar Michael could almost imagine his mother standing in the room with them, ready to rummage through her belongings. He shivered uncomfortably and adopted a logical thought – *it's probably grief* – yet the feeling was so strong. Not wanting to appear paranoid, he quietly told Bill, he'd wait outside.

Standing next to his vehicle, Michael rang Ryan. 'Hey, mate, you'd better come here if you want to see this house I think the old man's going to buy. I just want your endorsement. I reckon he's ready to take out the cheque book.'

'Where is he now?'

'He's still inside with the agent. I'll text you the address. Are you free?'

'Yeah, bro. I'll see you soon.'

Michael wandered around the yard and looked up and down the quiet street; he knew it would suit his father. At times like this, he tried hard to dispel any kind of sentimentality from his thoughts; he didn't want time to reflect or grieve. Outwardly, the house appeared much older than the house in Carinya but if this was his father's choice then let the process of purchasing it unfold.

Just as Michael was yearning to smoke a joint, Bill appeared at the doorway. He didn't look as cheerful as Michael expected, and he frowned. 'What's up, Dad? Are you all right?'

'Michael, I think it will always remind me of your mother. Nup, I cannot buy it!' He saw the pain come across his father's face and his eyes teared up.

'Okay, come on, Dad. Let's go home. I'll let the agent know while you drive. How about that?'

Bill looked relieved. Michael was the problem solver in the family, and driving back to the safety of the shed at Michael's was the best idea he'd heard all day. 'Too many ghosts, son.'

'Dad, I had a ghost feeling too whilst we were in the kitchen. That's why I went outside. And that friggin' bird put me off too!' They both chuckled at that. 'Look, just stay in the shed for as long as you like. It doesn't worry me at all. In fact, it's good to know you're around. Except for Mum, any ghost can piss off,' and they laughed easily again. 'Seriously, Dad, it could well be too soon. We'll just relax and let things take their course.'

Michael made the call to the real estate agent and smoothed over the situation with an apology for wasting her time. 'And, Dad, I think we'll put a tele in your shed too!'

Suddenly Michael remembered Ryan. He sent him a text. DEAL'S OFF. TALK LATER. A silence came between them and Michael watched the traffic speed by as Bill concentrated on his driving. Everyone seemed to be so purposefully engaged going somewhere or another, but soon enough they were home. 'Let's put the kettle on and make a brew. We'll sit near the fire if you can bring some wood in.'

The two men kept each other busy with menial tasks designed to stop them thinking and brooding. *Time will heal,* they kept telling themselves, and soon Ryan was coming up the side path, ready to join them.

'What happened?' he asked.

'Too many ghosts.'

'Have you got three mugs instead of two?' Ryan expected the situation to be awkward, but no words were needed.

'Dad's staying in the shed for a bit.'

Bill busied himself with the fire. 'Lots of kindling and paper make a good fire.' The two brothers looked at each other knowingly. Bill needed to be occupied.

'You organise the tea, Dad. I'm going to make a phone call outside with Ryan.'

The brothers stepped outside and sat on the verandah chairs. 'I'll make this quick because it's freezing out here. Firstly, can you organise a website for our glass-bottom boat? You'll need to investigate licences and liaise with our mate Patricia from the shire. She'll put you in touch with all the right people.'

Ryan scratched his head, swallowed hard and looked at Michael.

'Look we need to ensure it can be done before we start wrecking the boat. It won't turn into a new boat overnight, but we need to be sure we have procedures in place.'

The light faded from the day and traffic could be heard far in the distance. *Life just keeps on continuing*, thought Michael. 'Look we'd employ a web designer, but Patricia will help you with all the technical bits. And the kid down the road is starting his own business in computing so perhaps we could tap in there … help him out too, financially.'

'What's that kid's name? I've seen his ads in the paper.'

'Look, Ryan, it doesn't matter what his name is for God's sake!' Michael could feel the exasperation rising in his voice. There was a reason he regularly got mad with his brother. 'Look, are you in or out on this project?'

Ryan answered on cue. 'Of course, I'm in! Just settle down, will you? No need to get in a huff.' The brothers realised the tension in the air and the drizzle of rain didn't help. It was getting late and they were tired.

'Sorry, mate.' Michael knew his brother could do the business management and deal with all the complexities involved. He should have been a bit more sensitive, he realised. 'Bit of shit going down lately. I'm a bit edgy. Anyway, great if you could do that while I deal with Dad.'

'What needs to happen with him? I suppose he needs to get a semi licence, along with all his house hunting.' Ryan took a deep breath.

'Hey, I'll look after Dad, the licence and where he lives. Good to see you get started on the red tape involved with the new boat venture. That's going to be massive.' Michael suddenly felt like he had the weight of the world on his shoulders. He shuddered and pulled his hood over his head to keep his ears warm. He could smell someone's dinner cooking, probably next door, and it reminded him of another job he had to do. *God, if only I could employ a housekeeper too*, but he knew he was dreaming. He'd have to heat up a pizza again and go food shopping in the morning. Or perhaps Bill could have the job. *He could contribute*, Michael thought. 'Look, Ryan, let's have a beer near the fire before you go home. Is Emily waiting for you?'

'Yes, she probably is,' Ryan mused quietly. 'Look no hard feelings about my outburst. Just still a bit on edge, I guess, what with Mum going and Jodie missing. Sometimes I still feel like packing it all in.'

Michael did something he didn't normally do. He moved towards his brother and gave him a quick, solid hug. 'You'll make it. We'll all make it. Just a bit tough at the moment.' He could sense his brother's fragility. 'Look, you go home, bro and look after our precious Emily. Are you okay?' Michael didn't want Ryan to break down; he had enough to deal with. And Bill was only part of the issue. 'I'd better go and sort out the old man. Hopefully, he hasn't burnt the house down.'

They chuckled and remembered many times in the past when their father had been too exuberant, burning leaves swept up in the garden. Jane had stopped him and limited him to burning off only in winter. 'Good luck with your friend Patricia!' Michael teased.

Ryan began his walk towards the path. 'Hey, she's your friend, not mine,' and he smiled inwardly at the image of Patricia. 'Say goodbye to the old man for me.'

Ryan remembered the young blonde who worked for the shire – Patrica. She was 'ten out of ten' cute but at the time, Ryan had been happily married to Jodie. For the first time in many months, Ryan felt a stirring in his loins and realised he was close to being back in the dating game. He made a mental note to check the rings on her fingers when he spoke with her next, and then realised he wanted to begin the new boat business as soon as he could. He would visit Patrica in the morning to set up an appointment for their discussion. Ryan almost skipped down the wet path before getting to his car, blissfully unaware of the slipperiness of his actions. He didn't want to fall over or slip backwards, not when he'd just had the first glimmer of hope in many months.

'Your tea's cold, son. But at least the fire's going. Isn't it a beauty?' Michael smiled to see his father engaging fervently with the most banal activity! 'I'll make another cuppa for you and put the pizza in the oven.'

Bill began to leave the room. 'Is Asha on lates again? That's good, really. Gives us a chance to talk.'

Dad's old habit of answering his own questions, thinking aloud and producing the responses he wants to hear, Michael nodded inwardly.

'Yeah, put the kettle on and the pizza in the oven.' Michael thought about allocating the task of meals to his father but reneged on the idea. His father had been a rotten cook when they were growing up and he suspected things had changed very little. Jane had cooked right up until her passing. Michael still remembered the tap he'd turned off and wondered if she'd still be alive if he hadn't done so. A lump formed in his throat, so he swallowed hard and directed his benevolent thoughts to plans for his father.

'Dad, you know if you just stick to Heavy Rigids you won't need to sit a test? Your farm truck licence will cover you amply. And I really don't think you should be driving Heavy Combinations at your age. And Garry rarely ever has a need to transport that sort of stuff. It'll save the medicals and all the crap that goes with it.'

'Bugger it,' Bill replied. 'Maybe you're right. But maybe I should run it past Ned next time I see him.'

'No, Dad! Don't ask Ned anything; in fact, loosen all ties with him. He's sneaky, Dad. I know you might see him when you collect all your tools and equipment from your shed but hey, I'm not too keen on the old Ned. And I'm not sure if Lola's any better. You know, he hasn't earned the nickname Nosey Ned for no reason. Just be aware.'

Bill had heard this advice before, but from his perspective he hadn't any reason to dislike or mistrust Ned Lawson. However, he would heed his son's advice, and tried to remember which friend had also warned him against Ned. He left the room when he heard the kettle boil and guessed the pizza would be ready too.

'Actually, Dad, speaking of sheds, I have an idea.'

Bill continued cutting the pizza and pouring milk into the teas. 'Here's some for Asha too.'

Michael waited for his father to finish serving dinner, ensuring he had his father's full attention. 'Dad, what do you think about the idea of renovating the back shed so you could camp out the back here? I could hire a storage unit at the marina for all my gear. At this time of year, I could book one fairly easily. Then I could do all my work close to the boat.'

Bill's eyes brightened instantly. 'What a brilliant idea, son!' Now he wouldn't have to find another house. He would be close to Michael. God forbid, he could even cook dinner occasionally for the three of them. He didn't want to get ahead of himself but his response to Michael, and the expression on his face, left Michael in no doubt about his father's feelings. All the Thompson men went to bed happy and contented that night. Their problems were solved.

Chapter 22

An Informant Reveals

Ryan's serenity didn't last long! He'd slept well for the first time in months and woke feeling refreshed, smiling to himself when he thought of seeing Patricia. *Crikey, I hope she still works at the shire. I sure as hell don't want to deal with some boring middle-aged bloke who can only think about retirement and his pension.*

As he dressed with Patricia in mind, the phone rang and he felt annoyed that it had interrupted his pleasant thoughts for the day. He looked at the caller ID but didn't recognise the number, and begrudgingly answered it as he wandered up the passage towards the kitchen.

'Ryan Thompson?'

'Yes.' Immediately, Ryan's nerves steeled at the authoritative tone of the voice.

'It's Detective Stone from Port Burnie. We spoke before about your wife's disappearance.'

'Yes,' Ryan replied, aware they had spoken several times, each time leaving him convinced he was in deep shit. His stomach tightened now and sweat formed on his forehead.

'Mr Thomspon, I think you'd better come down to the station. We need to discuss a few things with you.'

Ryan almost dropped the phone. 'What? I'm just getting my daughter ready for school ...'

'Okay. After that will do. I'll be here till mid-morning.'

Ryan's mind ran wild, and his hands started to tremble. Without hesitation, he rang Michael and informed him of the call.

'Get Emily off to school and I'm on my way,' Michael said, 'and stay calm, mate.'

Michael's Landcruiser pulled up as Emily walked out the front gate. She waved cheerily to him as she turned left and strolled towards her school, looking quite the young schoolgirl and obviously unaware of the trauma that might be coming their way. Michael thrust his hands into his trouser pockets to keep warm and hurried along to the back door. 'Get the coffee happening, Ryan,' he called out. 'We need to get a few things straight before we head off.'

Michael pulled the door open quickly and let it bang shut behind him. 'Firstly, you need to assume your phone is bugged. Secondly, be careful of what you say when you get there. I reckon they are wanting to rattle your cage again, so don't give him any reason to do so. Take care, bro, take care. Plenty of innocent blokes in jail.' He flicked the kettle on because Ryan hadn't yet moved.

The coffee machine brewing relieved the tension in the kitchen and even the cat knew when to disappear as Ryan's despair continued. Michael noted his brother's shaking hands.

'Hold it together, Ryan. If they see you like this, they will take it as fear that they are onto you. Come on, take some deep breaths. You haven't done anything so you have nothing to fear.'

Ryan did as requested, and felt only slightly better – Michael wasn't the one being held under suspicion. They dallied long enough for Ryan to settle again, then Michael drove him to the Port Burnie Police Station, where, straight away, the detective ushered him into an Interrogation Room. He indicated the chair Ryan was to sit in. Sliding a folder on the table, he himself sat and fixed a stern stare on Ryan.

'I'll come straight to the point,' Detective Stone said. 'We have received information from a reliable source in Carinya that you put a hit out on your wife. Would you like to comment on that?'

Ryan's jaw dropped open, closed and opened twice more. He shook his head and his heart started thumping in his chest. Sweat broke out on his forehead again and his hands automatically started shaking. A cold chill washed over him. After a long pause, he shook his head again. 'No. Never. That's absolute bullshit!'

'Our source is trustworthy, Mr Thompson. We have no reason to dispute the information.'

'No. No … I'm not … I didn't do anything. Jodie was playing around. She often stayed out overnight but she always came home again. Just this time she didn't. Maybe she's still with whoever she was sleeping with … it's just a matter of time before she comes back.'

Detective Stone tapped a finger on the folder. 'Well, she hasn't yet, Mr Thompson. We also heard that you were at risk of losing a lot if she filed for divorce …'

'I was prepared to fight that … and fight for custody of my daughter.'

'Come on, Mr Thompson. You really believe the court would give you custody over the mother?' His eyebrow rose at Ryan's ludicrous suggestion. He sighed as though frustrated. 'Well, we are furthering our investigations. It is only a matter of time before we find her. I don't need to tell you not to leave town, do I?'

***

Back in the car, his hands still shaking, Ryan rehashed the conversation to Michael. 'Someone in Carinya has it in for me, Mike, and I don't know why. What have I ever done to someone in Carinya?'

'What have you ever done to anyone?' Michael retorted. 'All I can say is, they are stabbing in the dark. The statistics show that it's often the woman's partner or husband so they're still watching you and trying to rattle you into doing something stupid. They'll be watching your bank transactions and your daily travels. I wouldn't be making any moves at this stage on the gorgeous Patricia either. It could be construed as motive for getting rid of Jodie. I'm even paranoid enough to think our conversations are bugged!'

Ryan nodded. Indeed, Michael was becoming paranoid but he had a point. He wanted to change the subject so his brother didn't keep ranting on about it. He needed time to settle and stop his hands from trembling. 'It was lucky I didn't go to the shire office today. I was just starting to feel ready to move on, but hey, I'm going to be a monk from now on.'

Michael laughed and Ryan felt himself relax. 'Look, I'll be all right. I know I need to be, and Emily will be home soon.'

'Righto. I'll go see how the old man got on dealing with Garry and getting some work. There's a lot to take care of on many fronts, so I don't need you to muck up, bro,' Michael said and playfully hugged his brother. 'Just remember everything I've said. And remember to feed your cat, too, and I'll go home and feed mine.'

Michael wished feeding the cat was all he had to deal with, so he braced himself as he drove home, mentally preparing to deal with his father.

Chapter 23

Bill Severs Ties with Carinya

A week later, Bill once again drove along the road between Port Burnie and Carinya, and this time was surprised to see Ned at home and not parked on the road somewhere.

'No patrol duty today, Ned?'

'Nah, things are a bit quiet lately. I might go out later tonight if there's nothing on TV. One of the perks of the job is the flexibility.' He shrugged and grinned snidely. 'I love just popping up anywhere, anytime … puts the whoops up them all.' He chuckled at his own joke and Bill merely nodded. 'Anyway, I've got a house to pack up. You know what it's like moving house.'

Ned continued raking leaves, which was one of his favourite occupations when he was home, and Bill understood why he'd earned the nickname Nosey Ned – he was always watching. *Probably clocked up his gardening as overtime when he raked leaves on the weekend. Log it in as surveillance*, Bill thought, remembering everyone's opinion of the man.

'I've just come back to remove some things from the shed and sort out some of Jane's stuff. I stored a number of boxes in the back section, and I guess I'd better take them out of your way,' Bill called as he closed the car door. Colleen had told him the deposit had been paid into Bill's bank account so the place was now half Ned's.

'Don't worry on my account, Bill. You can leave them there for as long as you like.'

Bill felt a wave of friendship sweep over him and the feelings of mistrust Michael had warned him about puzzled him. Ned propped his rake against the wall and moved closer to the fence. 'Look, don't worry about paying the post office to redirect your mail either. I can get Lola to do that. No point paying extra is there?'

Bill nodded appreciatively and waved an acknowledgement. Then he took his key from his pocket to unlock the shed but, as he drew nearer, he saw it was already unlocked, which surprised him. *But then again, Ned is the new owner.* Most of the items in the boxes were Jane's and he didn't really know what to do with them. Leaving them here in the shed seemed a great solution, and if he wanted a drive in the country to get away for a while, having boxes here in the shed could serve as a suitable pretence. He'd thought of telling Ned he'd come and collect his mail from time to time but soon realised asking Lola to redirect mail was a much better idea.

***

While in Carinya, he had lunch with John and Fay and decided to delve more forcefully into John's warnings about Nosey Ned. His stomach rumbled as he rang the doorbell of John and Fay's home – breakfast seemed so long ago. Soon they were seated around the table eating corned beef encased between thick slices of fresh bread.

'Are you staying in Carinya overnight, Bill?' Fay asked.

'I think so. I'll doss down on a mattress in the shed out the back of the old house.'

'But hasn't it been transferred to Ned?' John's eyebrow rose. Then he frowned, and Bill took the opportunity to ask about Ned. He laughed a little in answer and nodded politely.

'Ned won't mind. The place is in midway – not fully paid for so we share until it is. Look, I've always found Ned okay, but I know it's not a popular opinion. What do you guys know that I probably should?'

For a moment, Fay and John stopped eating and glanced at each other. No one spoke, then John rose from his chair. 'Would anyone like anything else to eat?' He went to boil the kettle while Fay finished her sandwich. Behind Bill's back, John looked directly at Fay and kept his eyes on her as she wiped her mouth with a serviette. For Bill, it was clear they didn't want to talk about Ned so when John asked how things were proceeding with life in Port Burnie, Bill allowed the conversation to divert, which was more comfortable for all concerned. They spoke more easily with the tea in front of them, and when Bill's account of recent life concluded, he naturally asked about their work.

'I've got a few trucks outside in the shed if you want to come and have a look. I've reconditioned one for a bloke in New South Wales who's coming here next week. Then I've got a few truck audits to complete before the end of the month. It's all about compliance, and Fay has compliance forms to submit before long. She does the paperwork and I go out on the jobs.'

John led Bill towards the back door and into his enormous shed which housed a plethora of engines and paraphernalia pertaining to vehicles of all descriptions. 'I have dealings with Ned when there's been an accident. Sometimes I pick up smashed cars with the tow truck over there, and assess the vehicles for insurance purposes, and Ned fills out forms too.'

This was the most John had ever revealed to Bill so he was surprised to see a massive operation hidden within the shed. As they moved between vehicles, John murmured something Bill couldn't quite hear. Then he lowered his voice and leaned in closer to Bill. 'I think your boys are wise when they shed doubt on Ned's honesty, but I can't say anything more, except listen to your kids.'

Bill stood still and froze. Slowly, John moved away and strode towards the truck he'd been working on. He stepped up into the truck and opened the door, signalling for Bill to jump in beside him. Soon, there was so much noise conversing was impossible but from John's facial expression, Bill could see a happy man in his shed. A sense of normality was present, and this pleased him. Eventually, the key was turned off and John called out as he jumped from the running board, 'Let's go inside for a beer!'

Away from Fay's earshot, Bill asked the question that had been rolling around in his mind. 'So what do you think about me throwing down a mattress on the floor of my old shed?'

John laughed. 'Are you frightened of ghosts, mate?'

Bill relaxed and half smiled. Was it Jane that had caused him to ask that question?

'You can chuck down a mattress on the floor here after we've had dinner and watched the footie if you like. I'm sure old Ned wouldn't mind one bit.'

But Bill felt okay, now enveloped by the good friendship he'd known for so long. He wouldn't impose.

Many hours later, he dossed down on the shed floor, after leaving his car at John's and walking to his old home. Fay had promised him breakfast so he couldn't see the point in driving there and back.

An unfamiliar car was parked outside Ned's place when he arrived, so, to give Ned his privacy, he trod softly along the path that marked the territory between the two houses. He needn't have bothered as he could hear the television tuned in to a TV drama and assumed Ned was out. When Ned was home the television was only ever tuned to sport.

Without any more thought, he pulled up the rug John had given him and ignored his cold feet; he felt relieved to be out of the cold wind that now whistled around the corner of houses and the shed.

At some stage, loud male voices arguing outside Ned's house woke him, and, after his initial annoyance, Bill became curious and listened to the hostile situation. They were arguing about money, which made Bill even more interested. A voice he didn't recognise told Ned he wasn't leaving until he'd been paid. The ranting and swearing went on, Bill now wide awake and listening intently. *Who in their right mind argues with a cop? And, more to the point, why would Ned owe anyone any money?* He heard the back door open and Lola entered into the argument.

'GO INSIDE AND MIND YOUR OWN BUSINESS!' Ned shouted at her with no attempt to lower his voice at that hour of the night. The sound of the back door slamming echoed through the neighbourhood. Then it slammed again, which Bill presumed was Lola flexing muscle, so who knew what would happen next? The loud voices became muffled but remained hostile.

Under normal circumstances, Bill would have phoned the police but what was the point! Besides, he wasn't going to make a move and reveal his presence. He quickly assumed other neighbours would be privy to the raucous voices too, but it remained dark and motionless in the streets of Carinya, with only the testosterone-driven outburst disturbing the peace.

A heavy thumping along the path soon sounded and then, from the front gate, the stranger yelled, 'I'll be back when you've got my money and when you're not wearing your cop's uniform. Mark my words!'

A car door slammed. The driver tramped his foot, and the noisy engine roared as he drove away, tyres screeching as he sped around the corner.

Bill climbed back onto the mattress and eventually drifted back to sleep but he couldn't help reliving what he'd heard during the night. After a few hours of restlessness, he decided to return to his car at John's under the cover of darkness and, for a moment, wondered if he'd had too much to drink and perhaps had dreamt the whole thing. Then shook his head. No, he was quite certain about what he'd heard. He slipped his shoes on and bundled up his mattress and sleeping bag as quietly as he could, feeling lucky that he'd found the camping equipment so easily in the dark. He dared not click the shed lock and, knowing Ned hadn't been locking it, he felt relieved as he'd worried about becoming a prisoner in his own shed.

Sneaking along the side path, he stepped over the fence to avoid the gate groaning under sufferance. Darkness prevailed so he stood a while to let his eyes become accustomed to the blackness. Even the streetlights were out in sleepy Carinya and he didn't want to disturb a dog and cause a rumpus. He watched carefully for dips and holes in the footpath and soon John's street came into sight. He felt exhausted but knew he had to keep striding along the deserted road, pass a few more houses till he could see his car parked in front of John's house.

Towards the east, the sky tinged with pink and Bill realised his sons must see daybreak most mornings when they went fishing. *No wonder they are tiring of it.* But for now, he made his way to his car, pondering on seeing if John was awake so they could enjoy an early cheeky cup of coffee before he headed back to Port Burnie. He wasn't quite in the mood for sorting out Jane's boxes just yet. *Yes, John's kitchen light is on. No other houses have lights on. Trust John to be up early.* Bill could almost smell the coffee percolating and a smile wrinkled his face. *Coffee*, Bill thought, but, as he edged closer, he realised John's car wasn't there. *Where on Earth has he gone?* He opened his car door, and folded himself down onto the leather seat. *Perhaps he left early to finish a truck audit, but that's highly unlikely.* He remained puzzled and felt so tired he could easily have nodded off, but his adrenalin had kicked in as he pondered his friend's whereabouts. From his car, he could see Fay moving around in the kitchen and remembered no one in the country pulled their blinds down at night, but there was no sign of John or his car. By now, Bill was on high alert, his heart working overtime. He decided to creep closer to the house and discretely observe Fay. Dressed in a winter dressing gown, she was eating toast and reading the paper so clearly there was no emergency. But it didn't explain John's whereabouts at such an early hour.

He retreated to his car and remained silent. Birds were waking up and starting their early morning vigil, their noisy squawking soon to wake the townsfolk. If he wanted to leave unobtrusively, he needed to leave immediately. *Start the car!* But he knew Ned could soon be on the road trying to catch blokes who'd had too much to drink the night before so he quickly wrote a note and left it in the screen of the front door, apologising for skipping out on breakfast, then he turned the key and, as quietly as he could, cruised down the street and out of town.

For the duration of the drive, Bill kept thinking about Ned, and then about John and his whereabouts so early in the morning. Slowly, the pink sky became crimson and dawn broke. With the unexpected events in Carinya, he looked forward to surprising Michael with this newfound knowledge. Michael would be shocked too.

Chapter 24

The Bank Statement

Michael wasn't shocked at all. 'Look, Dad, I told you not to trust Ned. Others in town aren't going to say anything, are they? And who could they say anything to?'

Bill decided not to divulge his further concern over John's disappearance so early in the morning. He'd already detected the slight annoyance in Michael's voice. At the rate things were playing out, he didn't want Michael to think he was being paranoid.

'Also, Dad, I think it's too early to deal with Mum's clothes and other items in the boxes. Her whole life is in those boxes and, at some stage later, you and I can do it together.'

'Yeah, you're right,' Bill said, and breathed a sigh of relief.

'For now, we need to think about converting the shed into a bedsit for you. I'll get started on it today.'

Michael knew he sounded too authoritative and he made a mental effort to control himself before he uttered words. He began clearing up breakfast dishes as Asha appeared in the doorway, yawning. She moved towards the coffee machine after greeting Bill and hugging Michael as she brushed past him.

She's a great girl, Bill mused, and she reminded him in many ways of Jane. She was like a kind, little angel.

'Dad, did Ned *offer* to re-address your mail? Is that what you said?' Michael didn't like the idea of that, but was mindful of his father's fragility and didn't want to boss him around. 'He doesn't know our living arrangements.' He shrugged. 'But then, Nosey Ned knows everything, I guess. Let's focus on other things.' He changed the subject. After the day he'd had with Ryan, he too felt emotionally exhausted. He liked the way Asha simply found a chair at the table and took care of herself. *Low maintenance,* which totally suited him. He watched her meticulously spread marmalade on her toast, and soon she'd make a cup of coffee for herself and asked others if they'd like one. *She's a keeper,* he nodded, his heart swelling with gratitude. Her long hair hung beautifully, framing her face, and her manners at the table were classy. *I need to smarten myself up*, he considered and made a mental note to spoil her as much as he could. She brought out the romance in him and he was surprised to admit that he probably loved her.

'Are you on late shift again?' He liked the way she looked up at him and smiled as she answered the question. He knew the answer, but he just wanted to hear her voice.

'I love late shift. Nice and quiet. Not many dramas either in recent times but I'd better not pre-empt what could happen.' She returned the marmalade to the pantry as she looked knowingly at Michael. They smiled at each other, and Bill felt like an intruder. Eventually, she sat down and turned her gaze to her plate in a bid to consider the third person at the table.

Bill pushed his chair back and moved towards the door, declining a coffee as he rose. 'I'm going to the marina to see if I can catch up with Garry.' This would give his son some privacy. Besides, he felt like he needed a bit of space himself.

He looked forward to the shed conversion when he could feel it was slightly more like a home. Without Jane, life wasn't the same and he knew he'd have to learn to enjoy, or at least accept, his own solitude. Feeling slightly despondent, he drove on, looking forward to doing some work. *I just want to drive the truck and feel productive … feel I have a sense of purpose.*

***

That afternoon, Donna arrived home and quickly began to prepare the roast lamb for tea, Bill and Garry's favourite. The weeks since Jane's death had crept past slowly and gradually Donna found herself less immersed in her memories of Jane. She assumed this was the nature of grief – one of the stages. Would the pain lessen as time moved on? Perhaps. She wondered how long it would take before she could live a day without painful memories. It had been three months since the funeral. Each time she was about to wallow in self-pity, she thought about Bill and wondered how he was coping. She would ask him tonight at dinner but suspected the loneliness was dreadful.

It wasn't long before she heard the front door opening and men's cheerful voices filling the space in the Marshal house.

'You don't need to take your boots off, Bill.' Donna turned around in the kitchen in time to see them moving down the passage and, once all the greetings were finished, the men sat together in the lounge and began talking.

'So, Ned offered to redirect your mail, eh? Simply to save you a few dollars at the Post Office?' Garry took a deep breath and chuckled. 'The Neds of the world don't do anything without a good reason, mate.'

Bill listened to the same sentiments expressed by Michael, all the while knowing he'd stuffed up and reasoned he was just too ready to accept a hand of friendship from his neighbour. Evidently, it was a neighbour no one liked, or at least no one trusted – Bill was discovering that on many different levels. Yet, he had known nothing of this while Jane was alive. It was a mystery to him, but he sat back in his chair prepared to, reluctantly but politely, listen to Garry.

'So has any mail trickled into Michael's letterbox?' Garry reluctantly posed the question. He didn't want to cause Bill any further angst, but sometimes Bill was just so naive, it infuriated him. *Bill always believes the best in people, which perhaps is the reason I ended up being his brother-in-law. Jane chose well*, Garry decided.

Bill nodded and said slowly, 'I've received quite a bit of mail, mainly concerning Jane's business. She belonged to a few organisations, so I've been corresponding with them, letting them know things.' Bill blinked as he looked over at Garry. 'Actually, now when I think about it, I haven't heard from the bank. I'm surprised. I'm sure Stan would inform his staff of Michael's address.'

Then time stood still as Bill pondered the matter. 'I guess I haven't informed any organisation of Mike's address so the Post Office would send all mail to our Carinya home.'

'So, what I'm hearing is that your bank statement has been lost somewhere in transit? Or Ned is going to redirect it … Of course, he is!' Garry's jaw set, at which Bill frowned. 'Bill, you need to ring Stan in the morning and redirect your mail. They can issue another one, and there's always internet banking, but it still poses a question. Is all your mail being redirected or only some?'

'I'll drive to Carinya tomorrow and go to the bank; Stan will be there, I'm sure, so I can ask him to direct my mail to Mike's. I might see Ned too and pick up any mail that's sitting there and some of my boxes. I hope he's home.' Feeling suddenly anxious, Bill realised he was muttering his thoughts aloud.

***

In the Carinya bank the next morning, Stan thrust his hand out in greeting. Bill shook it and immediately felt relaxed. They hadn't seen each other since the funeral, and Stan noted Bill looked thinner, his face gaunter and his eyes had sunken somewhat into his eye sockets. However, his smile was friendly and as broad as ever. They had the necessary conversation, and the appropriate bank statement was printed.

'This would have been mailed to you,' Stan said, looking at the long column of figures on the paper. 'I'll check the outgoing mailing list for the last few weeks to confirm if it did actually go in the mail.' He entered another office nearby and reappeared fifteen minutes later. 'I've checked and rechecked. That statement was mailed to your old address here in Carinya about a month ago. Ned's had plenty of time to redirect it to you, particularly if he's redirected other mail.'

Stan frowned and his lips tightened as he looked hard at the statement. 'Look, Bill. Let's just go through those figures. Jane kept this account active right up to her passing and that's why statements would be mailed out until such times as we go through the formal closure of accounts, using the Death Certificate. It involves paperwork with the executor of the Will, which I assume … is you? I've been expecting you to come to close the account.'

Both men adjusted their glasses as they began to seriously assess the figures on a page. Stan waited, deliberately hoping Bill would identify the anomaly.

'Here we are in March. The withdrawal of a large sum — $9,900. Uh-oh, here it is again a few weeks later.' Bill stared hard as the words spilled from his mouth. 'Two separate cash withdrawals.'

'Jane came to see me about this. I endorsed the withdrawals, but I did think it was a bit strange.' Stan paused. 'Then I heard about her illness and assumed she wanted to give it to Ryan and Michael. She might have even said this – I can't remember – but I do know she justified the reason for the withdrawals.'

Bill shifted in his seat and felt confused. Why hadn't Jane made some reference to the money? Or had she and he disregarded any talk about money as he'd been too concerned with her health? He shook his head, totally awed by the withdrawals. 'This is all very stressful. Jane must have given it to the boys,' he muttered, not totally sure of his sentiments.

'Look, stay here and I'll make us a drink. Don't go away, Bill.' After a few minutes, Stan returned with two shooter glasses of brown liquid. 'Bugger the coffee, Bill. This calls for something stronger.'

The two men sipped at the cool liquid and soon the alcohol slid smoothly down their throats. *Stan's right*, thought Bill. *Bugger the coffee!*

'Bill, it's all part of the grieving. They say it takes a while to process.' Stan's words became blurred in Bill's mind as he assumed they were words of comfort and condolences in his rhetoric. He really felt like another drink but was astute enough to realise a bank manager and his client consuming alcohol on a working day wouldn't be endorsed if Head Office paid them a visit. *Bugger the reason.* As Stan's words concluded, he recognised Ned's name amongst the blur so he needed Stan to repeat what he had to say about Ned.

'You need to ask Ned why he didn't forward the bank paperwork to you when other mail was forwarded.' *Here's someone else making disparaging remarks about Ned and it certainly does require an explanation.* Bill shook his head, unsure if he had the courage to confront Ned, as he'd not forgotten the angry words he'd heard in the middle of the night, to a stranger who threatened to return and wreak havoc. *Ned sounded pretty scary! But then again, he is a cop. But he shouldn't be scary*, Bill reasoned internally.

He left the bank and drove around to the old house and was relieved to see the police patrol car missing from the driveway. *Good, he's out!* Relieved, Bill walked quickly down the path and into the shed to retrieve a few boxes to put into his car. As he entered, he cast his gaze around the shed and there, on a box, was a pile of letters and he wasn't surprised to see they were addressed to him. *No doubt Ned's going to take them to the mailbox soon.* Bill decided to take them to save Ned the trouble of re-addressing them and put the mail in the car along with the boxes.

As he sat looking over the mail, he saw one from the bank. It was a statement and it was obvious the letter had been opened. It was the same statement they'd just discussed in Stan's office. *So why had Ned opened his mail?*

Instantly, the hair on the back of Bill's neck stood up, and his heart raced as all the words of warning from others echoed in his head. Luckily, he was sitting down as his legs started to shake, maybe from anger at Ned's audacity, maybe from fear of his reasons. He felt suddenly nauseous and wished Jane was alive to help him deal with this dilemma. Minutes roared past, and still the sleepy town of Carinya remained unmoving. After some time, Bill decided to replace all the mail in the shed, and wait and see if Ned forwarded the opened letter from the bank. He unclicked his car door as quietly as he could and strode down the path towards the back of the house. His hands shook so much at this latest infuriation that he could hardly open the door, but he did, and placed the mail back where he'd seen it. He looked around furtively; not sure why – he hadn't done anything wrong.

Feeling ill, he walked as fast as he could back to the car, opened the door and turned the key in the ignition. With the engine humming, he began the sojourn to his new home, albeit a shed in Port Burnie. There was some comfort in knowing he'd be with Michael soon. Suddenly, he felt old and useless.

Chapter 25

The Surveillance Plan

Ned felt slightly irritated when he returned home for dinner after a call-out on the southwest road where there'd been a fatality. Two vehicles had collided and people were taken away in ambulances. Luckily, he'd been first on the scene, and had administered first aid without the interference of know-it-all onlookers. He'd quickly called the ambulance and then called John for the tow truck. Following the distressed sounds of someone calling out, he'd quickly administered first aid there, glancing occasionally at the other poor woman, the driver, who was slumped over or impaled on the steering wheel with blood streaming out. Clearly, loss of blood had caused her death and Ned felt relieved when a siren screamed in the distance. *Soon, someone else will deal with the death and dying*, Ned thought.

After dinner, Ned went to John's place where they began to write up the police reports and information for the insurance company.

'I'll add a few hours to the job,' he told John. 'There's always provision to stretch the number of hours worked on a job – you never know when other things will crop up that we haven't accounted for. You can add a few hours too.'

John shot him a stern glare. Indeed, Ned often added quite a few hours to insurance claims, particularly on weekends when overtime was paid, and he sometimes signed off without John's signature. If it *was* needed Ned just wrote John's name in the box on the form. Some people would call it forgery but, in Ned's mind, it was fair. No one really knew how long he'd been on a job if he was ever audited. He didn't see it as falsifying claims, but he soon refrained from involving or discussing it with John.

'I hear Bill Thompson's going to start driving trucks for a living,' Ned said as they finalised the documents. 'He was down on the weekend and I asked him what he'd been up to.' Ned always washed his car at John's workshop while he clocked up his time on the job, an activity that annoyed John no end. As Ned swept the floor of his car, he asked John what he'd been up to, but John was always evasive. Soon, conversation ceased and John went inside his house, leaving Ned to complete his car wash alone.

'No doubt about Ned. He's out there washing his car on taxpayer's time,' John told Fay as he sat down and undertook his own paperwork. 'What a user. I can't stand being around him.'

'Don't worry about him, love,' Fay replied. 'He'll fully slip up one day soon, particularly now he's so close to retirement. He'll make a mistake and reveal himself and fall for more than insurance fraud and forgery. You mark my words.' They ate dinner and watched television, both lost in their own thoughts about Ned Lawson.

'Did you let him know you were going to Port Burnie to do some truck audits in the morning?'

'Nope. The less he knows the better.' John went into his office and opened his filing cabinet, flicked through his files and soon the name *Ned Lawson* appeared, stuffed into the section in the locked cabinet entitled 'Police Surveillance'. He didn't have strong evidence but knew about Ned's history, and John's real task in Carinya was to monitor Ned's actions and record, where possible, evidence of corruption that would stand up in Court. The big boys wanted him, but he was small time and slippery. John, working undercover, dearly wanted to nab Ned before he retired, but the evidence had to be a lot stronger when there was a police uniform involved. John had watched and videoed Ned at the annual speedway event, and he'd installed CCTV in many places around town, but all he'd gathered so far was low-level thuggery and rubbing shoulders with the wrong element at best. It would be Christmas soon and Ned's retirement would probably coincide with the end of the year. He would like to think Fay was right, that hopefully he would reveal himself somehow, but time was fast running out. He thought of ringing Bill so they could have lunch together while he was in the area doing pseudo-truck business, his excuse for being on the road regularly to watch Ned's activities.

'Hi there, Bill …' Fay heard John on the phone. She was pleased he'd kept in touch with Bill and realised his loneliness after Jane's death had been enormous. She, too, missed her friend.

'Is lunch tomorrow good?' asked Fay when John entered the kitchen. John nodded and sat down ready to drink his tea.

'He's taken a job driving for his brother-in-law. But yes, we're having lunch at the pub.'

***

The Port Burnie Last Drop hotel was busy and loud, and Bill and John strained to hear each other as they tucked into their fish and chips.

'I wonder how many here are doing drug deals,' Bill wondered aloud between mouthfuls. 'Lots of blokes, I reckon. Mike said this is where he used to get his supply. All I can say is, I'm glad he's off the stuff.' He put down his fork and picked up his beer. 'He's taken up with this gorgeous lass, Asha – a real model of perfection – enough to make me laugh really, her taking up with Mike! I wish Jane could look down and see him. For the first time in a long time, he looks real happy.'

John smiled as Bill chuckled with contentment. 'Mike's a good bloke, and so is Ryan,' he commented, nodding; he had known them both for years.

'A bit of friction going on now with them, though. Just brother stuff from time to time.' Bill paused. 'Michael keeps telling me not to trust Nosey Ned, and you wouldn't believe what happened just recently. It was pretty bad, but I don't dare tell Mike or he'll hit the roof.' Finishing his meal, Bill wiped his mouth with his serviette and looked around. Then he lowered his voice and told John about finding his mail from the bank, opened by Ned.

'So, you had your letter from the bank and you could see it had been opened?' John nodded, one eyebrow rising. 'And this was in your shed?' John looked astounded, then his expression hardened. 'Did you ever receive the letter resealed and redirected to Mike's address?'

'Yep', replied Bill.

'You know it's a criminal offence to open other people's mail? It's hard to prove, though, so it rarely makes it to Court.' John shook his head and muttered something about Ned's integrity. 'What we need is evidence that holds up in Court.'

'Oh I don't think we need to take it that far,' Bill objected.

John scoffed and looked away, deep in thought. 'That's not the half of what he's been up to, I can tell you.' He caught the surprised look on Bill's face, and felt it was time to come clean. 'Look, Bill,' he said, lowering his voice, 'I'm an undercover cop. I've been placed in Carinya to bring Ned down. We have a heap of stuff on him but just need more concrete evidence to pull him down.'

Bill's eyes had widened and his jaw had set. 'Now that clears up a lot of the confusion I've had over you …'

'Well now you know,' John said nodding, 'it's critical you don't blow my cover. As always, the less you know the better. Not a word to anyone.' He stood and stretched. 'Leave this business with me and I'll come up with a plan to ensure it doesn't happen again. Let's meet this time next week as I usually do business in Port Burnie on a Friday. I'll text you during the week with a location. Not here – too many eyes.'

The next moment, he was gone and Bill was left sitting with his drink at the table. He looked around and didn't see anyone he knew, which was good.

***

A week later, they had lunch at the Wisteria Cafe and ordered sandwiches and coffee. 'No prying eyes here, Bill. Just a heap of women and I don't think they're planning any deals.' Just as a precaution, John scanned the café's interior as he sat down. Bill also noticed John always sat so he faced the doorway. *It must be a habit of a lifetime*, he thought.

'So, what's happening at home, mate?' John picked up the menu and pretended to read it as he glanced intermittently at Bill, waiting for an answer.

'Big week, but thank goodness, life seems to have settled down. Ryan is coping much better after the Police accused him of contracting a hit on Jodie …' His brow furrowed slightly when he said that and he went on slowly, 'and now he and Emily seem to have a good routine.' He took a deep breath, and seemed distracted momentarily. 'Thank goodness the family live close by so Emily has babysitters all the time.'

'Awful business with poor Ryan. He needs to stay alert, though, as he'll be the prime suspect until she's found and it's proven otherwise.' John continued, 'What about you, Bill?'

'My shed's looking more like a home. The kitchen's been installed so I make my own meals. It gives me a lot more independence. Tradies are working on the shower now. I have a portable loo, like the ones on boats. Michael's sorted me out real fine.'

Bill munched on his sandwich and ordered a second cup of coffee, then said, 'He's rented a shed near the marina and the boys work on the boat each day. They're converting it from a fishing boat to a tourist boat and they're surprised at their progress. Lots of red tape involved.'

'I can imagine.' John sat back and took a deep relaxed breath and then looked at Bill as he rummaged in his backpack. He took out a ticket and gave it to Bill. 'This is a bus ticket to Carinya on Sunday, if you choose to give me a hand to nab Ned Lawson. When you arrive, I want you to unobtrusively get yourself to my place. Your car can't be seen in town.'

Frowning, Bill looked at his ticket and placed it in his pocket.

John continued. 'Wear one of those windcheaters with a hood so you won't be recognised. You'll be officially undercover, Bill. I'll leave that part to your common sense.' John smiled thinly and cleared his throat. While he sounded calm, inside, he was conscious of the extra adrenalin rushing through his system as he remembered watching deals go down at the speedway on the night he'd found a contact for Jane for her to get some pain relief. So much more had been going down that night.

'Listen up, my friend. I've been watching Ned for a long time and I know his habits. He's using your house, by night, to meet his dealers. He needs it close to his house and away from Lola.'

Bill sat up straighter, remembering the rage in Ned's voice when he screamed at his wife to go inside on the night he'd slept in his shed, and he listened more attentively as he knew he'd have a part in this unwanted dilemma. 'Go on, John!'

'You've still got your outside key under your side gas bottle?' John read Bill's face – the key was still there alright. 'Well, Bill, I need you to install the mini-cameras for CCTV inside your house. We'll do it Monday morning when I know Ned will be on the road.'

'Whoa, John! What if he catches us?'

'Bill, he won't. And don't forget the house is still legally yours. I'll be on the street watching for him. He won't return and even if he does, you can get into the shed when I contact you.'

Time stretched on, and Bill's world rocked. He sat in the café, stunned. Others moved around them, oblivious to the serious conversation happening at the table near the window. 'Bill, I'll show you how to set up the cameras on Sunday night. Too easy.'

John read the hesitation on Bill's face and had prepared for what he needed to say. 'If we don't nail Ned, I know he'll have Ryan arrested on charges pertaining to Jodie. We know he's waiting for Ryan to make a wrong move. He's been stirring the pot a bit with the Port Burnie D's, and I even heard he'd put his hand up to work on the Jodie Thompson case.'

Bill stiffened, then froze. 'Hell!' he replied and then tried to relax again. He didn't want to draw attention to himself in this little café. He tried to process what he'd just heard but his heart thumped so loudly he felt sure others would hear it. John, however, merely sat there and looked out the window from time to time.

'I know this is another world for you, Bill. We need to carry through with this, so I'll see you on Sunday – at my place. I'll have a beer ready for you, mate.'

With those comments, John placed a reassuring hand on Bill's shoulder, then left the café. Bill was left mulling over all John's recent words. Yet other words were prodding his brain. Finally, he paid for his meal on his credit card and left the building.

Chapter 26

Truck Driving

After his weekend stay with John, Bill returned to Port Burnie, relieved to know John's plan was in place. He'd undertaken the installation of the cameras in each main room, his hands sweating throughout the procedure. He'd learnt a lot during the weekend, including that he'd make a bloody lousy detective as he'd leapt every time Lola slammed her back door. Being on the bus gave him a long while to process the last few days. During the journey, his whole body relaxed and he realised the strain he'd been under while at John's, but he had to do it to protect Ryan from Ned's fabricated rumours. That news had rocked his whole world. Now, he just wanted to get home and get back to work for the distraction.

All too soon, the bus arrived at Port Burnie and Bill walked home, backpack and all, feeling the distance, fresh air and the exercise did him the world of good. He'd undertaken a lot of walking on the weekend as he moved between his old home and John's. And that had cleared his head too. Hopefully, he'd sleep better now he was away from Ned's territory.

Once again, the proximity to Michael's calmed him. For now, he just yearned to keep his head down, and enjoy the solitude provided by driving a truck.

Michael heard his father dawdling along the path and recognised the tiredness. 'Dad, where've you been?'

'I caught the bus to Carinya and stayed with John for the weekend. I'm a bit tired so I think I'll go straight to bed.'

Immediately, Michael recognised something different in his father's behaviour. *And why didn't he take the car?* He would have discussed this with Asha but she was working. *Oh well,* he thought, *I'm not his keeper.* And he went into his office to update his paperwork until Asha unlocked the front door. By then he'd forgotten about Bill and only had eyes for her.

The next morning, Michael left his father sleeping undisturbed and drove to the marina to continue working on the boat. Ryan was already there so he made a mental note to ask for an update on the website. Already he'd forgotten about his father's strange behaviour.

The conversion from a fishing boat to a tourist boat turned out to be relatively straightforward and they were now only waiting on special hardened glass to arrive from overseas. 'So, Patricia was helpful, was she?' Michael asked.

He nodded, smiling subtly. 'She was amazing, Mike, and what a looker! No rings. But, with the Jodie business still hanging over me, I'm not pursuing it.'

'Mate, you can always look! But I know what you mean. You're under close scrutiny I'd say. The cops probably know when you sneeze!' They were still contemplating the opposite sex when Bill arrived.

'Well, well, well. Look who's here!' Ryan called as a greeting. Soon cheerful exchanges were taking place in the comfort of the marina shed.

'Great spot, Mike. So close to the jetty. I can even hear the water lapping up on the sand,' Bill exclaimed.

'Glad you like it, Dad, coz I put your name, along with mine, on the lease. That way you can use the showers, the gym and they've even got a storage area for trailers or boats. Very generous, I reckon.'

'Good idea. I'll use the showers as the tradies are a bit slow installing the bathroom. Saves me using yours. I know you don't mind but I wouldn't like to walk in on Asha.'

Michael waved an arm to dismiss the thought. 'She uses the hospital facilities before and after work. Saves transferring germs, she says, and she's probably not wrong.'

Bill made himself a cup of coffee. 'Love the idea of being self-contained. Someone could almost live here. Perhaps I should stay here instead of in your shed.' Bill sat down and stretched out on the chair. 'Nah, just kidding. I like it at yours, Mike. Someone's gotta look after me.' He grinned wryly. 'Actually, talking of looking after each other, we need to have a talk about your mum's estate.'

The mood changed from jovial to sombre and the boys slowly put their tools down and hesitantly joined their father for morning tea. Ryan took a biscuit from the packet and passed them around. Bill paused with his coffee and looked at his sons quietly and contentedly.

'Firstly, both of you. Did your mother give you a lump sum of money before she died?'

Bill noticed each son look from one to the other and shake their head. 'It would be good, Dad, but the answer's "No" from me.'

'Nor me,' Ryan added.

It was a simple question for his sons but their answers had massive ramifications. *So where the hell did the twenty grand go? What did she do with it? Maybe she stashed it somewhere amongst her stuff and it's now sitting in the shed at Ned's.* He dragged his fingers down the sides of his mouth, then ran his hand through his sparse hair. *What the hell did she do with it?* He exhaled deeply, something prodding him deep in the back of his mind; something Jane had said a long time ago that he had forced himself to forget. He almost shook his head as a cold chill washed over him, and, noticing the boys look at him strangely, moved the conversation on as smoothly as he could. He explained how joint accounts were dealt with in the Will and stated that he'd been to see Stan at the bank. What he didn't mention was his dealings with John – that topic was strictly off-limits. For a fleeting moment he felt like he was living a double life and then realised he was, and smiled. He was certainly going to keep a closer eye on Ryan, for Ryan's sake. 'Well, let's move on now. I'm glad you're both here.'

The regularly occurring pressures of debt and finances always underpinned business, and the boating world was no exception. 'Quite simply, boys, would you like me to contribute some funds towards your new venture? You can make me your silent partner, for tax reasons, and now I also have funds from the sale of the Carinya house. What do you think?'

Michael's and Ryan's eyes widened. 'Dad! …' they chorused together, 'that'd be fabulous!' Then they started jabbering about how the money would help. Bill thought they sounded like kids at Christmas time, then remembered them as children. Of course, they were always going to be kids to him and he smiled inwardly. He felt light-hearted for the first time in months and thought perhaps life was going to be okay after all. He relished the moment and smiled widely at his two sons' happiness. Caught up in the moment, he suddenly felt young again instead of old, which had come to serve as his constant companion in recent times.

'Let me know too if you'd like me to do the books. It'll save you time and, let's face it, you certainly don't want to employ anyone if you don't have to. Oh, I could contribute half the funds if you like and then you two could go halves in the remainder. Give it some thought.'

Although Bill loved the moment, he knew he needed to leave his sons to get on with their work. 'Anyhow, I've got a truck to drive, so I'll see you later.' With that parting comment, he drove away from the marina.

'Great to see the old man happy, isn't it? Such a bugger of a year for him and for you, too, bro.' *It's been a rotten year for all of us really, but Ryan's doing it tougher than most, and no wonder with that friggin' detective hanging around Ryan like he's a criminal.* A million thoughts ran through Michael's head and he realised the roller coaster of emotions was starting to send him loopy.

'Why don't we throw a party for the old man? We could ask all those awesome cousins who come on Christmas Day and make it a bit of fun – we'll celebrate Christmas early.'

Ryan didn't look impressed by his idea.

'Come on, bro. We could borrow a boat and catch some crayfish. The patch up near Boggy Bay is always a good spot this time of year.'

Ryan continued painting.

Michael looked at his sad brother and thought, *Look we're going to do something for the old man. And you're going to help me.*

***

When Michael arrived home that night, Bill was still in good spirits. 'After today's discussion, I bought a bottle of champagne to celebrate. Not sure what we're celebrating, but honestly, Mike, what a shocker of a year we've had.' Bill placed several champagne flutes on the table and held the bottle in his hand. 'I thought we could do with a bit of cheerfulness.'

'Dad, I totally agree. It's time for some good cheer. I was thinking of a party for your birthday and asking all the extended family.' Michael felt good to be away from Sad Sack Ryan, then instantly felt guilty for such thoughts. He acknowledged his own emotions were erratic and made a mental note to keep himself in check. He didn't want or need to go crazy! He could well do with some support, just like Ryan did, but Michael had to keep his cards close to his chest. No one needed to know a certain cylinder tap had ended his mother's life.

'Good idea, son. I'll ring Donna tomorrow. She knows how to throw a good party.'

'Call her tomorrow while you're waiting for a load,' Michael laughed.

'Yep. I'll be waiting for quite a few loads now, I bet. But that's what I want.' Bill looked happy and realised he'd been wanting something to do to put purpose in his life. He honestly hadn't felt useful since they'd sold the farm. 'Garry's got a few containers arriving in the next month and has booked me to do all his truck work. That's exactly what I want.'

'What about your bookwork for us?' Michael asked whimsically, then realised how petulant he'd sounded. 'Dad, only kidding. You can do the bookwork after dark if you get very busy or make phone calls sitting in the truck. Nothing like multitasking.' Michael picked up a champagne flute and examined it closely. 'Do we have to wait for anyone else or can we have a drink now?'

Bill popped the cork with finesse and filled the flutes. 'Here's cheers, my boy! Let's toast the future with our partnership.' They both sipped gratefully. 'Where's Ryan?'

'When I left, he was finishing his painting. He'll probably need to go home to Emily. No time for messing around with champagne. He's pouring himself into his work, Dad.' Michael chuckled at his own joke, but Bill wasn't listening.

'Mike, shall we set up a desk at the back of my shed? I can make that section into an office.' He was seriously intent on his new mission in life.

'Good idea, let's do it now and then I can throw some steaks on the barbie for us. You can finish off the details while I prepare a salad to go with the steaks.'

Bill chuckled to himself, amused at how Mike thought his idea about dinner was original. It was the same process almost every night. Steak on the barbeque with a salad. Still, they both liked their routine and it was easy, particularly considering Asha ate dinner at the hospital nearly every night. Bill enjoyed a few hours with his son and was sure it was mutual. After eating they usually went their separate ways – Bill to his shed, Michael to his house. The arrangement suited them both.

Later, Michael helped Bill arrange his filing cabinet and personal papers. Among the accounts, he noticed the bank statement Stan had given Bill at the bank and rather nonchalantly glanced at the figures. *This is Mum's final bank statement.* On closer inspection, he noticed the two cash withdrawals and his jaw dropped open. *Is this what Dad had referred to today?* The whole notion of his mother giving either Ryan or himself such a huge sum of money was incomprehensible. It just didn't make sense. He remembered how quickly it was dismissed during the conversation earlier and here it was again, popping its head up.

Totally perplexed, Michael decided not to worry his father at this point, particularly when he was cheerful for the first time in months. He put the bank statement aside, along with other papers, in the middle of his father's desk and went back to his own abode.

Chapter 27

Jodie is Found

The next day, all hell broke loose in Port Burnie. The radio headlines announced: 'A decomposed body has been found in dense woodland in the Cleland National Park. Police are investigating the disappearance of several missing persons and opening cold cases in the hope of making an identification.'

Ryan was only slightly distracted by the news report as he prepared Emily's breakfast, but was more distracted by his phone suddenly ringing. He picked it up as he poured hot water into his coffee cup.

'This is Ryan,' he said cordially.

'Mr Thompson, this is Detective Stone …'

Straight away, Ryan looked at the radio on the shelf. A cold shiver swept up his spine.

'Yes.'

'We'd like you to come down to the station …'

Ryan sank into a chair, and glanced at Emily as she came into the room from the passage.

'Dad, you look white,' she said bluntly.

Ryan tried to catch his breath, tried to get his heart beating again. He wiped his face. He could feel himself trembling.

'I need to get my daughter off to school.'

'That's okay, Mr Thompson. We can wait.'

He could almost see the detective sneering that they had him. Of course, they could wait!

He tried to stay busy, packing Emily's lunch, brushing her hair, giving her a prolonged hug as he sent her out the door, praying no one at school would tell her a body had been found. *Is it Jodie? Maybe it's not Jodie! You haven't done anything so don't be so scared. Shit! ... Shit! Shit! Shit!*

With Emily out of hearing range, Ryan rang Michael. 'Did you hear on the news ... they've found a body?'

'Yeah, I heard, mate. But don't panic ... it might not be Jodie. There's been a few missing people in the last eight months. It could be any one of them.'

'Yeah, I told myself that too, but the D's rang and want me to go to the station. I'm real worried, bro.'

Michael sighed deeply, gathered his strength and authorative tone. 'They want you down at the station ... we'll that's a good sign, mate. If it was Jodie and they had anything on you, they'd be bashing down your front door.'

Ryan felt the cold chill dissipate slightly. *Of course! Mike's right ... they wouldn't let me be wandering around in case I shot through.* He breathed easier. 'I'm heading down there now then,' he said with bravado. 'They're probably calling in relatives of all the missing persons. Yeah ...'

'I'll meet you down there,' Michael told him. *Brotherly support and all that,* he griped. *Who knows what hell this day is going to bring.*

When they arrived, Ryan was again ushered into the Interrogation Room, leaving Michael out in the foyer. Detective Stone again indicated to Ryan to sit in a particular chair, then sat on the opposite side of the table.

As he placed the folder on the table in front of him, he looked up at Ryan and said, 'Ryan ... is it okay if I call you Ryan? ...'

Ryan stiffened but nodded, immediately noting the change in the detective's tone. He eyed him with suspicion.

'Right … Ryan, you may have heard on the radio that a body was found yesterday in the National Park about two hours from here.'

Ryan continued to look at him, waiting … waiting for the accusations … waiting for the questioning. He relaxed slightly, knowing there was no reason Jodie would ever go there. So the body wasn't Jodie; he could breathe easy. Which he did, taking in a deep breath and letting it out.

'We are interviewing all families with missing family members in order to find out who this person was. If you are agreeable, I would like to show you some photos of the clothing the deceased was wearing. If you recognise it, it might bring this case quickly to a close … after DNA testing to verify …' He looked up at Ryan '… if you know what I mean …'

Ryan could imagine but didn't dwell on it. It wasn't Jodie.

Detective Stone slowly opened the folder and slid out a couple of large colour photos, which Ryan simply glanced at. *Jodie would never wear that awful colour,* he thought, glancing again at the image of a stained brown t-shirt. He went to look away, but something pulled his gaze back; he tried to look away, suddenly realising the brown was probably decomposition. He started shaking his head, stopped and started shaking his head again. *No, it isn't … it couldn't be … No, no, no …* But there, distinctly through the stained fabric, was the faint image of Mickey Mouse giving the finger – her favourite t-shirt.

Even though he was sitting, his legs felt weak and he buried his head in his hands. And kept shaking his head.

Detective Stone slid the photos back into the folder. 'You recognise the item?' he asked calmly.

His hands still covering his face, Ryan nodded.

'You are aware this only steers us towards further investigation … forensic investigation,' he added, still speaking softly.

Ryan nodded and slowly looked up. Tears were in his eyes. 'I'm sure that is my wife's,' he said, trying not to image her body lying in the morgue or on a steel forensic table. Then a thought jabbed into his mind. *I'll be arrested next. Someone said I put a hit on her.* He shook his head again, expecting, waiting for those words he often heard on TV … 'Ryan Thompson, we are placing you under arrest for the murder of your wife.'

'I didn't do it,' he said aloud, staring at the floor.

The detective heaved out a deep breath. 'We know.'

Ryan looked up suddenly. *They know?* 'You know who did it … whatever they did …? What happened to her?' His voice grew louder.

'Calm down, Ryan. We can't give you further details until we are sure it is your wife, but foul play is suspected. And we need to follow up on those reports that indicated you put a hit out on your wife. For that reason, the less you know the better at the moment.'

The detective rose from his chair. 'If it is Jodie, I am sorry for your loss. It is wise now to go home with your brother and wait for us to contact you. We'll let you know when we have more information.'

He opened the door and let Ryan into the corridor. Michael stood at the end of it, waiting, scrutising their expressions, their body language. His shoulders slumped on seeing Ryan's moist eyes. *Shit!* As Ryan entered the foyer Michael's open hands silently asked the question.

'I think it's her,' Ryan told him softly.

'And?'

Ryan sighed. 'I don't know how, but they know I didn't do it,' he added quietly. *Indeed, how do they know I didn't …* His heart thudded dully with all the unanswered questions.

Michael followed him home in the car and as soon as they were inside, opened the fridge, which, at this time of the week, was almost bereft of food. However, there was a carton of eggs so he took them out and prepared an omelette. A few minutes later, he slid a plate down in front of his brother and then made coffee.

'Here, an omelette each and a cuppa. Then we should go and get Emily and break the news to her.'

Ryan shook his head. 'No, we won't say anything right away as we don't really know for sure it's Jodie.' It was more to try and convince himself it wasn't her.

"Well, don't forget to log a timeline of your movements on the day Jodie disappeared. I hate to say it but ensure you have plenty of witnesses and alibis in case they can't come up with whoever did this. You will still be next in line.'

****

A few days later, Ryan still felt totally shattered. Each time he drew in a deep breath, the air tasted warm and foul. His tongue stuck to the roof of his dry mouth, and he found it difficult to swallow. He put his face in his hands and, deep within his chest, he let out an animalistic scream until his lungs felt ready to burst. He then remembered to shut the back door to remain silent to neighbours. He sat down again and looked around, his vision still blurred from his tears. He went into his bedroom, and flopped onto the bed and ultimately surrendered to sleep.

He didn't know how long he'd slept, but he woke with a start and instantly reached for his phone on the dresser. He couldn't remember the last time he'd used it, and was not surprised to see he'd missed several calls. His message bank echoed words he dreaded to hear.

'This is Detective Stone. Can you call me on this number at your earliest convenience.'

Shit! The D's will think I've skipped! Immediately, he hit the redial button, and the call connected to the detective. At the end of the call, Ryan knew they had identified Jodie through her dental records, and that she'd been a victim of foul play. He replayed the conversation in his head, then wondered how he could have slept through his phone ringing. Then he realised it was still on Silent from earlier in the day when he just needed a break. He still felt exhausted and his task now was just beginning.

Emily would be home soon and he wondered how he was going to tell his young daughter that her mother had been found. Right on cue, the back door banged. *Emily!* He would need to talk with her. Slowly, he eased up off the bed, and sat, the movement draining all his energy. He listened to the patter of rain on the roof and smelt the dampness drifting through the open window. His heart skipped and thudded as he prepared himself for the most difficult task he'd ever have to undertake.

Ryan made his way slowly to the kitchen and slumped into a cold steel seat. She read his face instantly.

'Have they found Mum?'

'Come here, Em. Come and sit with me.' And Ryan began and finished his story, telling her only that she'd been found. And the little girl sobbed into his shoulder.

Chapter 28

Ned's Rage

Ned had been keeping a close watch on the Police reports going through the system since the finding of a body in a National Park hours away from Carinya. He'd had a strong suspicion that Ryan Thompson had put a contract out on his wife … well, no, it wasn't a strong suspicion … he damn well knew it. And he'd reported that fact to the powers that be. But, for a while now, things had gone quiet – no more reports coming through the office.

Hurrying back from a routine 'welfare check' out to the Ferguson farm, Ned flicked a switch to the siren and cars instantly moved out of his way. The lack of reports coming across the register unnerved him no end. It was deadly quiet on the Jodie Thompson case, which should have been raving hot by now. *Why hasn't Ryan Thompson been arrested?!*

Soon enough, he turned the corner into his street, pulled up briefly and went into the stationhouse to check for any updated reports. *Nothing!* Then he drove past his house and parked outside the old Thompson house, which he now referred to as his 'other office'. He unlocked the front door, and plopped down onto a kitchen chair, took out his 'other' phone, and rapidly punched in a number. *Imagine the dilemma if I used the wrong phone for this! Imagine if I mistakenly used the police phone.*

God forbid! He shook his head to dismiss the thought and focused as the call connected.

Todd and Ron answered. They weren't their real names, of course – their real names were actually unpronounceable and much too identifiable, so Todd and Ron suited the situation.

'You two get your butts around here tonight. Actually, make it now and I'll wait for you here in my new office. Don't go to my house. Go next door.' He then hung up and walked to the kitchen, opened the fridge and took out a beer to occupy himself while waiting. *This thing is really turning to shit*, he thought. *I gotta make sure they did exactly as instructed …*

When he heard a car approaching, he opened the front door, seething. By the look on the men's faces, they knew trouble was imminent. Ned let them in and shut the door.

'Have you two totally stuffed up, or what?!' Ned bellowed as soon as they turned to face him. 'Did you follow my instructions? SUCH SIMPLE INSTRUCTIONS. Did you do everything I told you to do?'

Ned had worked himself up into a rage. If they hadn't obeyed him to the letter, not only were the men in deep trouble, but he was also in the hot seat – they could all, in a very short space of time, end up in jail for a long time.

'Jodie Thompson. You killed her. That's what I paid you for.'

Both men half-shrugged. 'Yeah. You paid … we did.'

'Was she dead when you left her?'

'She wouldn't last long,' came the smug reply.

Ned felt his lid about to blow if the next answer was as blasé. 'You took some of my stuff to do the job, didn't you! I told you … zip-ties, dark hood, tape and hessian bag. I'm missing a body bag and a set of handcuffs. Did you use my Police issued equipment?!'

Ned paced across the floor, then stopped and stared right into the men's faces, first one, then the other. 'You did, didn't you. And you didn't go back and remove the gear, did you?! You left it there, along with the girl, and now the gear is in the coroner's office ready for someone to trace it right back here.'

Ned's face had turned crimson. 'Am I right?' He stiffened. 'Everything will be traceable, or at least bring suspicion this way, given past history. You idiots! You might as well have offed her with my service pistol.'

The men glanced at each other but remained silent. In the distance, a dog barked, a car roared by, and a parrot made a racket outside. Ned hated them all. 'Do you know what? I feel like putting a hit out on you both to make you disappear.'

Both men attempted to talk at once but Ned shut them down, and silence reigned for a moment. Ned paced again, still in disbelief. And he thought it had all gone down so well. He hadn't fully recognised Jane Thompson's voice when she'd called for his services, but he hadn't missed her dropping the second payment off in the hollow tree in the park. He'd thought she was doing the drop for her son. That payment had been his share for being the go-between. The other two had shared the first payment. *What a pair of eggheads!* He paced again, an idea forming. 'What you two need to do is catch a plane out of here as soon as you can. Get out of the state, then out of the country.'

Relief flooded over Todd's and Ron's faces.

'Did either of you wear gloves on the job? ... No? ... Well guess what ... your fingerprints are probably all over the vinyl bag, all over the handcuffs ... along with mine. I can plead stolen property .. but you two ... well, you're dead meat. They're probably getting warrants for your arrest right now.'

Now the men looked as worried as Ned felt.

'Now get moving before I order a hit on you so you can't speak if they catch you. I expect you to be on the first plane or boat out of here. No excuses, as the story is already breaking on the News. JUST GO!'

The men pressed towards the door and fled down the path – they weren't hanging around in case he changed his mind. They hadn't returned to the crime scene to retrieve the gear as they never dreamed the body would ever be discovered so deep in the scrub. And now they needed to leave the country! They had no choice!

Those stupid sods! They've risked the network. As soon as the gang found out what they'd done, a hit would be put out on them, their petty crimes leading the law straight back to their associates. *And through them to me … and maybe there'd be a hit on me.*

Ned shivered and locked the front door. *Maybe,* he thought, *I can just stay home for a bit. I don't dare expose myself out there on my own, certainly not on a lonely road doing speed checks. Lay low, Ned, at least until Todd and Ron are on a plane out of the country. But how will I know?*

Slowly, Ned picked up his phone and moved towards the locked filing cabinet he'd put in Bill's old office. Retrieving the key from his pocket, he checked the phone to ensure it was the right one and placed it among his files. He wouldn't be using it for some time. Then he checked to ensure all his paperwork was in order and double-checked Jane Thompson's bank statement. It was there and clearly stated – *a sizable cash withdrawal.* When he saw her make the drop, he knew he'd need evidence to pin the hit on Ryan, with his mother as an accomplice, though she was out of the equation now. Anything to divert suspicion on himself. He turned the filing cabinet key, knowing all security measures had been adhered to, at least on his part. But the middle drawer kept dragging his attention.

There was a lot of money in a box pressed at the back of the suspension files. A lot of money. And he thought of adding the 'welfare check' he'd collected from Ferguson's farm that afternoon. He should add it to the box, but something gave him the jitters, so he left the large wad of notes in his breast pocket. The police phone remained on the table, so Ned sat down again, still seething, his mind in turmoil.

The Thompson's wall clock ticked monotonously and annoyed Ned so much, he wanted to rip it off and heave it. But he recognised his anger and remained seated, thinking. *Perhaps, I should apply for some leave and get out of town for a while. But then, with those idiots fleeing the country, maybe I'll get blamed in total. Maybe I should get out of here too.*

Police procedures scurried through his mind. The investigation had not resulted in Ryan Thompson behind bars, yet. Forensics had resulted in a positive ID, and maybe discovered prints and other DNA, though a long time had passed since the body had been dumped. *What evidence would be left? How much evidence would be retained inside the body bag?* So much flicked through his mind. Then he wondered how long it would take before a car appeared out the front to take him in for questioning. Of course, he could plead the equipment had been stolen … and they wouldn't trace any money back to him because he'd learnt not to put it into a bank account, which is how he'd been targetted last time. Oh no, all his cash, his regular welfare/protection payments from the illegal operations in town, his shares of every deal, including the latest hit, he kept in cash. Kept it under his nose, within easy reach. He glanced at the middle filing cabinet drawer. *What if they search the place? Do they even know I half own this house? What if Lola opens her big trap?* His ill-gotten gains were greatly at risk. He shook his head. *It's not worth the risk.*

And so he altered his plans.

***

Delighted by the idea of a holiday in a romantic location, Lola promptly packed her bags, no questions asked. Ned had insisted that they do this immediately and that if it didn't happen right then he could change his mind, so she packed only the bare essentials. He wasn't in a particularly agreeable mood, and hadn't been for some time, so she recognised he definitely needed a holiday. He wasn't interested in any suggestions she had, but, accustomed to following his orders, she obeyed. Playing the subservient wife was always her best option.

'I'll google some places on the way,' Lola suggested as Ned loaded suitcases into the family car in the driveway. Thankfully their passports still had a couple of years before expiry, and he would pick the first flight that had two seats available to a location that didn't require a visa.

He then parked the police car near the front gate so it was in full view. Unless someone inspected him closely, he appeared to be home. He also made Lola leave her phone behind, and turned it off, and did the same with his police phone. Then they headed out the door for their romantic holiday.

In the Thompson house next door, the middle filing cabinet drawer sat open, the box at the back of the drawer empty. Its contents were carefully layered in the bottom of Ned's flight bag, the one with the Police emblem emblazoned across it.

***

Garry and Bill sat shocked, and Michael expected as much. 'Well, Dad, it's not what you needed to hear so early in your new career.'

Bill squirmed in his chair. He tried to muster a chuckle at Mike's attempt at humour, and while appreciating the load being carried by his eldest son, he shook his head. 'Poor Ryan,' he said. 'Poor, poor Emily. I'm so glad Jane wasn't here to hear this.' Then he checked himself. Big withdrawals still prodded his conscience. *Where had the money gone?* He'd lay awake several nights after learning of the huge amount of cash Jane had extracted from the account, recalling yet disregarding her comments about a hit. *How much would it cost? Or should he ask, how much did it cost?*

Bill felt his stomach churn and his mouth watered as bile rose and then subsided. Garry and Bill remained quiet for a long time. Bill couldn't even imagine what Ryan and Emily were going through.

Finally, Garry said, 'I suppose, deep down, we've been expecting something like this.'

'Is Ryan home now?' Bill asked. 'He probably shouldn't be left on his own.' They were all lost in their own thoughts, knowing full well the fragility of Ryan's mental state. 'I'll go and get him. We need to keep him busy.'

Chapter 29

John's Phone Call

The warmth of the morning sun struggled through the glass of Bill's car window as he sat, thinking that it should be warming up now: it was late spring. He checked his briefcase to ensure all his documents were ready for the accountant. Yes, all documents pertaining to Mike and Ryan's new business were in order but there was one anomaly. Now that he was a silent partner, his financial situation came under scrutiny. How could he explain the huge cash withdrawal Jane made before her passing? The boys didn't know anything about it, so he was going to suggest to Steven that they leave that aspect until next year. His bones chilled at the thought of what Jane might have done; she had hated Jodie so much for what she was doing to their son and Emily. She had nothing to lose ... *But if she didn't, did she stash the money in the house he'd sold to Ned Lawson? What else could she have done with it?* This question would play on his mind until he found the answer. Would it make any difference to how he felt about his wife of many years? He didn't know.

Pushing his thoughts away, he reached forward to turn the key in the ignition when the phone rang. The caller ID indicated it was John.

'What's up, mate?' Bill said after he'd pressed the green button.

'Well might you ask! Lots.'

There was a pause and Bill sensed John was gathering his wits to talk. He heard a deep sigh. 'Bill, you'd better get here as soon as you can. I think Ned's done a runner but we'll talk as soon as you get here. I'd suggest you cancel your plans for today. This could be huge, but I need you here right now.'

'I'm in the car now. I've got an appointment with the accountant.' Bill's mind started to race, but all thoughts seemed to disappear in a fog – recently he'd found he struggled if he needed to act or think fast.

'Who's your accountant? I'll ring and get you another appointment, but I need you to get on the road now and come straight to mine.'

'Okay,' Bill answered tiredly. He'd been sitting, thinking about the huge sum missing from the bank account and wondering where it could be, and now, he had to focus on John and his current request.

Bill did as asked and was soon on the familiar road to Carinya … again!

This time, John was leaning on his front fence waiting for him. He opened the passenger's side door and slid in. The car engine hadn't even stopped. 'Righto, off to your old place, or should I say, Ned's new place.'

The car knew the road between John and Bill's house well; it was a road much travelled.

When they arrived, it certainly appeared both houses were deserted. 'The police car's in the drive, but I bet if you walk down your path and look through Ned's garage window, you'll see an empty garage.'

Bill noticed the locked padlock on Ned's garage and did indeed look in the window. John was right. Their private car was gone.

'Don't touch anything for the moment, Bill. We don't want to contaminate any evidence.' Bill hesitated and put his hands on his hips as he stood still. At this stage, nothing seemed out of place.

'What are we going to do?' Bill asked, puzzled.

'This is what we're going to do. I'm going to stay in the car and keep watch from a distance, just in case. Bill, my friend, you're going to get your outside key and retrieve the inside cameras.'

Sounds simple enough, Bill thought. 'I only have to remember where all those little blighters are.'

'Be as quick as you can. I'll keep watch. Just ensure your phone's in your pocket in case I spot Ned.'

John felt certain Ned would be absent for a while. Prior to Bill's arrival, he had phoned Head Office to get an update on Ned's suspected activities. Ned's location was listed as unknown, which was unusual; his phone wasn't answering. Most police officers informed the Head Office of their whereabouts when on leave or on a dangerous duty in case backup was needed. Not so, for Ned this time. Lola's absence, too, tweaked John's common sense about the nature of Ned's leave; they would be out of town for a while.

'Let's get those cameras out of the house as soon as we can!'

***

Later that afternoon, John uploaded the camera software onto his computer and into the folder labelled BILL THOMPSON. There were all the photos of the rooms in Bill's old house, just where the camera had been positioned to record. There was also a folder entitled NED LAWSON. 'You can see we've been tracking Ned for years, and do you know what? ... this time we've got what we've been waiting for, or at least I hope we have.' John's face lit up and he pushed aside a messy collection of papers on his desk.

Bill's eyes ran over the computer screen as John expertly pressed keys on the keyboard. Noises came from the kitchen as John focused on the computer, and the smell of coffee drifted into the office. 'I reckon we've nailed him,' John said again as he looked up at Bill's face with a wide grin. 'But I'm not going to get ahead of myself. If this software is working as it should, then we'll see and hear inside your lounge room. And *BOOM!* The evidence for justice will present itself.'

As John pressed buttons, Bill looked on astounded. 'But, mate, how can you be so sure?'

'Ever since you installed those cameras, I've been watching the place. When it hasn't been me watching, Fay has been. Your place has been totally under surveillance.' He smiled up at Bill. 'Yep, she's on the police payroll too. She's a federal undercover investigator and when there's a job on, there's a job on for both of us. We watch in shifts. Undercover work requires a lot of patience. Your info has led us to take this action. It's all documented and dated, Bill. That's our job,' John said pragmatically.

He paused as Bill took it all in, totally mesmerised. 'Now that I've told you all this, Bill, I need to lodge paperwork on your cooperation as a police informant. This is all with your consent, of course?'

All this time, John had been staring at the screen with his fingers expertly scrolling on the mouse.

'Unbelievable,' Bill murmured. He sat silently, realising how little he knew of his friend, and now realised his need for secrecy when they'd asked what he did for a living – the truck audits and maintenance was just a cover. He couldn't be sure, but he did know he wasn't going to question John any further to avoid undermining the operation. Indeed, the less he knew, the better. Like pieces of a jigsaw, Bill's mind sorted and placed the pieces.

'We'll do the paperwork later, Bill, but let's get this show on the road. Are you prepared to see your lounge room?' John didn't wait for an answer; he himself was anxious enough to see the footage. He pushed the Play button and watched as Ned appeared on the screen, walking around the room. Some time passed before the critical part of the CCTV footage featured. Bill watched, astounded how the footage could be paused, zoomed in, and then stopped to fast-forward to the time and action.

'The audio is perfect,' John muttered. 'Fay, come and look at this!'

The atmosphere felt taut with tension as they each watched the incident unfold on the screen. '*BINGO!*' John leapt up from his chair and raised his fists with excitement, as the evidence they needed for a conviction came on the screen. 'This is what we wanted but certainly didn't expect!' His eyes widened, and he peered more closely at the screen. 'Ned knew Jodie's killers! He supplied the tools to commit the crime. He knew about the hood and the handcuffs. And, from what he's just said, he *is* involved with gangs. Yahoo!' he shouted as he thumped the pause button and let out a massive sigh of relief. He turned a circle, hands on his head, realising the importance of what they had discovered.

An eternity seemed to pass as they sat contemplating the enormity of it all. Fay leaned over and pressed the Save button. 'Years of work!' she sighed, 'and now we have evidence.'

'I'm glad I bought those new cameras. We could have used the old ones, which record for twenty-four hours, upload the footage to a designated computer and then get wiped after a week if no one actively saves it. But the new cameras identify faces more clearly and give wider coverage in each shot.' John kept talking while Bill gaped at the screen. 'Also, the audio is better on the new cameras. Less crackling which the defence would use in their favour. There's no doubt about any of the images on this footage.'

John placed his hand on Bill's shoulder. 'Great work, mate. Let's go outside for some fresh air and I'll rustle up something to eat. Are you right to make the calls, Fay?'

An imperceptible murmur of agreement spread through the room, an invisible load disappearing like a puff of smoke as they made their way outside. Having sat still for so long screening the videos, their leg muscles had seized up like the trucks in John's shed. The warm day was a welcome respite after a long and dreary winter of grey days and frequent drizzly rain.

'One thing's for sure, Bill … Ryan's going to be relieved.'

Bill's voice was slow and raspy. 'Too right,' he said, nodding slightly, the skin around his neck suddenly moving as if it had recently received a good message from his brain. Bill turned to face them. 'He worried for a long time the cops would pin Jodie's disappearance on him.'

'Realistically, he had good reason to worry. The stats indicate it's usually the partner, and he was probably under surveillance all this time. Too funny … Ned would have been wanting to stitch him up!'

'I'm not sure. Ryan never said very much but I know he was worried.'

'Of course, he wouldn't know he was being watched. That's the whole point. Any decent detective doesn't blow his cover.'

John put down a plate of ham, cheese, and biscuits on the table. 'That's not enough for lunch. I'll go pick up a loaf of bread from the bakery.' A heavy-set man, John's boots could be heard stomping along the path to the garage.

Bill took the opportunity to quietly gather his thoughts and replayed the video images in his mind. He stepped towards the back fence and cast his gaze to the thick bush. The flies were just starting to become a nuisance and the odd mosquito buzzed around. Carinya was only a small rural town and Bill wondered if tiny insects were like the human inhabitants – necessary, but often noisy and a nuisance. Occasionally, the mosquitoes caused damage, and so too did the flies, but kept in check, normality reigned. He watched as a mosquito became caught in a spider's web, and despite the struggle, the poor insect couldn't resist the death throes. But today, here in Carinya, he had seen the dark side of some human inhabitants. Bill wondered if all folk had a dark side – perhaps only when sufficiently provoked, did the dark side appear. He was deep in his quandary when John's car returned.

'A crooked cop and his cronies, all ready to nurture crime and strike when prompted. A good job done here, Bill.'

John hurried inside and soon reappeared with cut bread, plates, and mugs of pumpkin soup. 'Come over here,' he called, jerking Bill out of his reverie.

'Where's Fay gone?' Bill asked, expecting her to appear and join them for lunch.

'On surveillance … checking up on other crims,' John said as he spread butter on his bread and cut the cheese.

Bill's jaw dropped. He was about to take a mouthful of soup but stopped midway to his mouth. 'Are you joking?'

'Quite a few people under surveillance here and we take turns.'

Bill shook his head in disbelief while John chuckled. 'Yep, but you don't want to know about it, remember?'

Soon, it was Bill's turn to chuckle and shake his head. 'Oh well, all I can say is how nice this fresh bread is.'

'When we've finished here, Bill we'll go inside and fill out some paperwork. Then, after you head home, Fay and I will mark up the footage and prepare to hand it to the crime squad as evidence. It's all very quiet, of course, so not a word to anyone, especially not to Ryan. We don't want Ned alerted at this stage, wherever he is. All low key, mate.'

As Bill drove away from Carinya, the sun sat high in the sky and summer was commanding a presence. He felt relieved to know Ned wouldn't be on the road ahead and relaxed, and assumed the habit of a lifetime – driving away from Carinya, albeit without Jane. It was almost his birthday, 16th December, and he felt relieved he could have a quiet time and just come to terms with the happenings of the day, his mind occasionally flicking back to the scenes of the CCTV.

Eventually, the town of Port Burnie appeared in the distance and he wondered how long it would be before Michael's shed became his home, and Carinya, with Jane, became a place in his distant past. *How many years will it take to assume my new normality*, he wondered.

Chapter 30

Christmas Again

'Bill, *you* don't need to take notice of bank withdrawals, regardless of amounts. Being in a savings account, tax would already have been paid before the money went in there. Certainly, the tax office won't be after you so rest easy – you are entitled to spend your money,' Steven reassured Bill, yet Bill still felt uneasy even though he had complete faith in the accountant. 'However, it does make you wonder what she did with it,' Steven added as he scanned the bank statement once again.

'Bill, perhaps we'll never know.' His laconic response hinted at a lack of interest, which pleased Bill. The bank withdrawal left in abeyance, Bill departed the accountant's premises as soon as he could. If he wasn't going to be pursued by the tax office, he was content and would happily leave all accounting until well into the new year. He breathed a sigh of relief.

For Ryan and Michael, the special hardened glass for the bottom of their tourist boat arrived from Germany and they busily installed it. Next, they needed to replace cleats and fenders, which required trips to the chandlery store. Seats needed installing and progress was underway for their purchase and fitting. Mooring lines and safety rails needed to be replaced to meet a safety audit, and that was next. Their website was established, and the technical support team had completed the software to enable bookings to start from the new year. Bill felt pleased; the boys were excited, and he secretly felt thrilled they seemed to enjoy working together at last. In the past, there had been occasional hiccups that needed regular smoothing, and Jane had largely been the one to ease tensions between them. The separateness of their roles would ensure harmony for their business, Bill hoped.

Truck driving for Garry suited Bill as he liked being close to the marina and he didn't have too much responsibility. After his short sojourn with John, he quickly established which drivers had clandestine activities running alongside their legitimate day jobs, and proudly reported in. John was correct when he'd talked about the amount of surveillance happening on the street and regularly wondered about the stray parked car with a quiet occupant reading the paper. He'd seen John often and the police raid on Ned was due to happen just prior to Christmas. He needed to keep his head down and his lips closed, which was easy enough to do.

'Christmas Day at our place again, Bill,' Garry said, mindful of not drawing attention to the family holiday time. With the absence of Jane this year; it would be painful. He made a mental note to consider ways, perhaps, to lessen the pain of absent friends, and involve Emily, too – he would talk about it with her.

Leading up to Christmas was a quiet time in the boat dock business, as most folk seemed to spend their money on Christmas or holidays.

'Why don't we ask everyone to propose a toast for the new year when we have the family for breakfast? Then we can extend it with the cousins when everyone comes for lunch.' Donna had been thinking about Christmas and, with the arrival of Lexie and Talia sometime soon, she thought she'd better have a few ideas in mind.

'I'm assuming you mean Bill and the boys, plus Emily, and the four of us?' Garry asked later that night after dinner. 'That's the breakfast gang, right?'

'Yes, and then later it may work, or it simply may become too rowdy for toasts. Depends how many turn up. We love the cousins, of course, but, being such an eventful year, who knows how it will play out?'

***

On Christmas Day the breakfast gang gathered early at Donna and Garry's where they smelt the bacon on the barbeque and heard Christmas Carols being played somewhere inside the house. Lexie and Talia were thrilled to escape the cold weather of Britain, though they were already booked on their return flights, to manage their work schedules.

Garry ensured everyone had a full stomach and before long, he had everyone gathered in some kind of circle.

'This year's been one hell of a struggle,' he said, 'but here we are. We've managed to be all together as a family for Christmas Day and we thought it'd be a good idea to make a statement of gratitude or propose a toast or simply say something positive as we move forward into the new year.'

He filled his champagne flute with bubbly pink liquid and raised it above his head. 'I love the idea of Bill being my new truck driver. Good on you, Bill.'

'Oh, I see what you need to do!' Emily said, delighted. 'Can I go next?'

Garry nodded happily and poured a tiny taste of champagne into a glass for her. 'I miss my Mummy. Nasty people stole her, but I am glad she didn't leave me.' She paused, her lip trembling. 'Merry Christmas.'

The family clapped and cheered. She took a sip of the precious liquid. 'Oooh, that is disgusting ...' she said, screwing up her face. She wiped her mouth, then said, 'Dad, can you go next?'

Ryan stood up awkwardly and hugged his little girl. He took a deep breath and looked from Emily to his family. 'It's emotional so I'll keep it short. Thanks to you all, and welcome home Talia and Lexie. I owe you both a beer.' He looked at his cousins and remembered the pain in the aftermath of his mother's funeral, and the pursuit by the police to find him guilty of murder. Quickly, he swallowed and made a concerted effort to smile as he sat down. 'I now nominate Lexie.'

'I've developed a fabulous vet clinic in the UK so I'm doing what I love. Who knows, perhaps one day I may develop one here in South Australia. Watch this space! Cheers! I nominate Talia next'.

Talia stood up and raised her rapidly depleting glass. 'Where my sister goes, I go. Very cute I know, but thanks to Mum and Dad – look at us all here and what beautiful food and people.' Talia looked towards her mother. 'I nominate Mum.'

Donna stood and, looking around, took a moment to reflect. 'I lost my sister this year but with the support of my gang here, I made it. Thanks to you all, and with that sentiment, I nominate Michael.'

'Thanks, Donna,' Michael said. He remembered the tap he'd turned off to stop the oxygen in his mother's room whilst she was on her death bed. He felt such gratitude to Donna for keeping his secret. 'What a year! So many moments to acknowledge without saying too much. We're lucky to have each other and I'm looking forward to a new boating venture. Also, now I can suggest a whole lot of new chicks for Ryan to chase. Block those ears, Emily!'

Michael looked towards his father and gave him a wink. 'I nominate the old man!' He knew he needed to keep the atmosphere light and breezy.

Bill stood up with a smile and paused before he began to speak. He raised his glass. 'Listen up, you lot!'

'Dad, that's what you always say. Let's hear something new,' Michael called out cheekily. 'What about some gossip!'

'You mean like you popping the question to the lovely Asha?' He gained immense joy from the look on Michael's face, and the pert smile on Asha's. 'Righto, you lot!' he went on, looking around. 'I have some more gossip so fill up your glasses and take off your hats.'

Bill clearly loved his audience ramping him up! 'Nosey Ned Lawson's been apprehended getting on a plane to Hong Kong, with copious amounts of cash.'

He stopped to allow his statement to sink in. This was the moment he'd been waiting for and what a wonderful way to impart the knowledge.

Michael stared hard at his father, wondering if he'd gone crazy.

As Bill looked around at his family, they were all mystified and looked at each other in total disbelief. They waited. 'He's been a crooked cop for a long time and recently has been setting up Ryan but now, son, rest easy. Ned's going to jail, for a long time.'

The Thompson and Marshal families looked shocked, wondering if Bill had lost the plot since losing Jane. 'I'm not going to get morbid, but Ryan, you can relax and move forward with Michael on your new boating venture.'

He paused and moved towards Ryan. 'I can't reveal my sources but trust me. It'll be in the papers shortly, perhaps during the week.'

They looked at each other and felt the heat of the day. 'People have been saying for years how corrupt Ned's been, but I couldn't see it. My neighbour! Now the proof is in the pudding, or his hand luggage. But the less said, the better!'

Each family member looked at him and Bill could feel the frown on his forehead deepen as he heard the emotion creeping into his voice. He didn't want to become teary or upset so he raised his glass a little higher. For several moments he didn't move from his place near the doorway. Even the crows were silent for a while.

'Okay, let's drink to all of us. And in particular to Jane and justice. Maybe she's watching from above and hopefully knows we appreciate everything she's done for us.'

'Here, here,' they all chorused. 'To Jane, and justice!'

About the Author

Lyn Bodycoat's career as a writer has evolved since finishing work as an English teacher in 2017. She currently supervises undergraduate and postgraduate teachers at a Western Australian University. She is an active member of the Society of Women Writers of W.A. and, in her spare time, she hones her skills as a writer.

This is her 4th publication with Linellen Press.